NOW *and* THEN

www.noexit.co.uk

NOW *and* THEN

ROBERT B. PARKER

NO EXIT PRESS

First published in the UK in 2007 by No Exit Press,
P.O.Box 394, Harpenden, Herts, AL5 1XJ
www.noexit.co.uk

A CIP catalogue record for this book is available from the British
Library.

ISBN 10: 1-84243-209-5 (hardcover)
ISBN 13: 978-1-84243-209-9 (hardcover)

ISBN 10: 1-84243-210-9 (trade paperback)
ISBN 13: 978-1-84243-210-5 (trade paperback)

2 4 6 8 10 9 7 5 3 1

Typeset by Avocet Typeset, Chilton, Aylesbury, Bucks
Printed and bound in Great Britain by J.H.Haynes Ltd, Sparkford, Somerset

BOOK DESIGN BY AMANDA DEWEY

This is for Rose . . . always.

1.

HE CAME INTO my office carrying a thin briefcase under his left arm. He was wearing a dark suit and a white shirt with a red-and-blue-striped tie. His red hair was cut very short. He had a thin, sharp face. He closed the door carefully behind him and turned and gave me the hard eye.

"You Spenser?" he said.

"And proud of it," I said.

He looked at me aggressively and didn't say anything. I smiled pleasantly.

"Are you being a wise guy?" he said.

"Only for a second," I said. "What can I do for you?"

"I don't like this," he said.

"Well," I said. "It's a start."

"I don't like funny either," he said.

"Then we should do great," I said.

"My name is Dennis Doherty," he said.

"I love alliteration," I said.

"What?"

"There I go again," I said.

"Listen, pal. You don't want my business, just say so."

"I don't want your business," I said.

"Okay," he said.

He stood and walked toward my door. He opened it and stopped and turned around.

"I came on a little strong," he said.

"I noticed that," I said.

"Lemme start over," Doherty said.

I nodded.

"Try not to frighten me," I said.

He closed the door and came back and sat in one of the chairs in front of my desk. He looked at me for a time. No aggression. Just taking notice.

"You ever box?" he said.

I nodded.

"The nose?" I said.

"More around the eyes," Doherty said.

"Observant," I said.

"The nose has been broken," Doherty said. "I can see that. But it's not flattened."

"I retired before it got flat," I said.

Doherty nodded. He looked at the large picture of Susan on my desk.

"You married?" he said.

"Not quite," I said.

"Ever been married?"

"Not exactly," I said.

"Who's in the picture?" he said.

"Girl of my dreams," I said.

"You together?" Doherty said.

"Yes."

"But not married," he said.

"No."

"Been together long?" he said.

"Yes."

We were quiet.

"You having trouble with your wife?" I said after a time.

He glanced at the wedding ring on his left hand. Then he looked back at me and didn't answer.

"The only person you could ever talk with is your wife," I said, "and she's the issue, so you can't talk to her."

He kept looking at me and then slowly nodded.

"You know," he said.

"I do."

"You've been through it."

"I've been through something," I said.

He looked at Susan's picture.

"With her?" he said.

"Yes."

"You're still together."

"Yes."

"And you're all right?" Doherty said.

"Very."

With his elbows on the arms of the chair, he clasped his hands and rested his chin on them.

"So it's possible," he said.

"Never over till it's over," I said.

"Yeah," he said.

I waited. He sat. Then he opened the thin briefcase and took out an 8×10 photograph. He put the photograph in front of me on the desk.

"Jordan Richmond," he said.

"Your wife."

"Yes," Doherty said. "She kept her name. She's a professor."

"Ah," I said, as if he had explained something.

I try to be encouraging.

"I think she thought it was low class," he said. "To have a name like Doherty."

"Too ethnic," I said.

"Too Irish," he said.

"Even worse," I said.

"I don't mean she's snobby," Doherty said. "She isn't. She just grew up different than I did. Private school, Smith College."

"Kids?" I said.

"No."

"Where do I come in?" I said.

He took in a big breath of air.

"I want you to find out what she's up to," he said.

"What do you think she's up to?" I said.

"I don't know. She's out late a lot. Sometimes when she comes home I can tell she's been drinking."

"Oh," I said. "That."

"That?"

"You think she's fooling around," I said.

"I don't think she'd do that to me," he said.

"Maybe it's not about you," I said.

"What?"

I shook my head.

"So what do you think?" I said.

"I don't know what to think, it's just not going well. She's out too much. She's sort of brusque when she's home. I don't know. I want you to find out."

There were a few questions I wanted to ask, but they were more shrink-type questions. And he wasn't hiring me for my shrink skills.

"Okay," I said.

"What do you charge?"

I told him. He nodded.

"And you'll find out?" he said.

"Yes."

"I don't want her to know," Doherty said.

"I'm pretty slick," I said. "Where do you live?"

"No need to know that," he said. "You can pick her up at school."

"And tail her home," I said.

He nodded.

"Of course," he said. "Six thirty-six Brant Island Road in Milton."

I looked at the picture.

"Good likeness of her?" I said.

"Yes," he said. "She's fifty-one, looks younger. Five feet, seven inches, a hundred and thirty pounds. She's in good shape. Works out. Drives a silver Honda Prelude. Mass plate number ARP7 JD5."

He reached into the slim briefcase again and brought out a printed sheet of paper. He put it on the desk beside her photograph.

"Her teaching schedule," he said. "Concord College, you know where it is?"

"I do."

"Her office is in Foss Hall," Doherty said. "English department. It's on the schedule."

"How about you," I said. "How do I reach you?"

"I'll give you my cell phone," he said.

I wrote it down.

"Where do you work?" I said.

"You don't need to know that," he said. "Cell phone will get me."

I didn't press it.

"You want regular reports?"

"No. When you know something, tell me."

"If she's doing anything out of the ordinary," I said, "it shouldn't take long to catch her."

He nodded.

"I don't think she's having an affair," he said.

"Sure," I said.

"When can you start?"

"I'm away for a couple of days," I said. "I'll start Tuesday."

He didn't move. I waited.

"She's not . . ." he said finally. "I can't see her having an affair . . . she's not that interested in sex."

"I'll let you know," I said.

He nodded and turned and headed for the door. The way his jacket fell, he might have been carrying a gun behind his right hip.

2.

IT WAS LATE SEPTEMBER on Cape Cod, and the summer people were gone. Susan and I liked to go down for a couple of nights in the off-season, before things shut down for the winter. Which is how we ended up on a Sunday night, eating cold plum soup and broiled Cape scallops, and drinking a bottle of Gewürztraminer at Chillingsworth in Brewster.

"When someone says that their mate is not interested in sex," Susan said, "all they can really speak to with authority is that their mate is not interested in sex with them."

"I've never made that statement," I said.

"And with good reason," Susan said.

"It sounds like sex to me," I said.

"And it sounds like he fears that it is," Susan said.

"He fears something," I said.

"And he's reticent about himself," she said. "Didn't want to tell you where he lived. Won't tell you where he works."

"Lot of people are embarrassed about things like this," I said.

"Are you?" she said.

"No more than you are, shrink girl."

She smiled and sipped her wine.

She said, "We both uncover secrets, I guess."

"And chase after hidden truths," I said.

"And people are often better for it," she said.

"But not always."

"No," she said. "Not always."

We ate our plum soup happily and sipped our wine.

"You don't like divorce cases, do you?" she said.

"Make me feel like a Peeping Tom," I said.

Susan smiled, which is a luminous sight.

"Is that different than a private eye?" she said.

"I hope so," I said.

"You feel intrepid, chasing bad guys," Susan said.

"Yes."

"And sleazy, chasing errant mates."

"Yes."

"But you do it," she said.

"It's work."

"It's good work," Susan said. "The pain of emotional loss is intense."

"I recall," I said.

"Yes," she said. "We both do. Half my practice comes from people like that."

"Despite similarities, our practices are not identical."

"Mine requires less muscle," she said. "But the point is, you can rescue people in different ways. Leaping tall buildings at a single bound is not the only way."

"I know," I said.

"Which is why you'll work divorce cases," she said, "even though they make you feel sleazy."

"Heroism has its downside," I said.

"It has its upside too," Susan said.

Susan's eyes had a small glitter.

"Speaking of which . . ." I said.

"Could we maybe finish dinner?" she said.

"Of course," I said. "The upside is patient."

"And frequent," Susan said.

3.

I KNEW Doherty's name and address. It would not be very hard to find out more about him. He had not, however, hired me to find out anything about him. So I decided to find out about his wife.

Concord College was not in Concord. It was in Cambridge. Three recent high-rise buildings with a lot of windows, just across the Longfellow Bridge in Kendall Square. A software tycoon with a streak of vestigial hippie-ness had endowed the place with a sum larger than the GNP of several small countries. And the college, perhaps respectful of its financial base, was an exfoliating swamp of unusual ideas. It cost about $40,000 a year to go there.

I went into Foss Hall, which was the middle high-rise, and up to the fourth floor. Aside from my adulthood, I was too neat to be mistaken for a student. Most of them wore very sloppy clothes that had cost a lot. Chronologically, I could have passed for faculty, but once again the neatness factor gave me away. The faculty was no neater than the students, but their clothes had cost less. Hoping to pass anyway, I was carrying a green book bag. Deep cover.

According to the schedule Doherty had given me, Jordan Richmond's office was in room 425, and her office hours began in ten minutes. I strolled past the office. It had an oak door with a window. There was no one in there. I wandered past the door and stopped to study a bulletin board, beyond the next office. *Crush Imperialism . . . Film Festival: Jean-Luc Godard . . . Stop the Murders for Oil . . . Roommate Wanted, M or F . . . Wage Peace . . . No Welfare for the Wealthy . . . Keg Party at MIT . . . African-American conference . . . Concordian Lecture Series: "Apollonian Despair in the Poetry of Sara Teasdale" . . . Equal Work, Equal Wage . . . Gay & Lesbian Coalition . . . Intelligent Design Is Neither . . .* Maybe it wasn't such a hothouse of new ideas. Except for Apollonian Despair. As I studied the notices, Jordan Richmond strolled past me down the hall toward her office.

Her picture didn't do her justice. There was a time in my life when I would have thought that admiring the butt of a fifty-one-year-old woman was exploiting the elderly. I had not entertained that conceit in some years, but if I had, Jordan Richmond would have ended it. She had brown hair with blond highlights. By the standards of her colleagues she appeared to be vastly overdressed. Glimpsed covertly as she passed, she seemed to be wearing makeup. She had on black pants and a jacket with a faint chalk stripe. Under the jacket was a pink tee. By the sound they made on the hard floor, I could tell she was wearing heels.

I hung around the hallway, trying to look inconspicuous, until she finished her office hours at 4:30 and, carrying a black leather briefcase, she headed out of the building. I went with her. We stood so close in the elevator that I could smell her perfume.

On the street we turned right and she went into the Marriott hotel. I took a baseball cap out of my book bag and put it on. Spenser, master of disguise. Then I put the book bag in a trash basket out front, waited for a moment, and went in after her. She was in the lobby bar. At a table with a man. I sat with my hat on, at the far end of the bar, where it turned. It put her back to me, and I could look at her companion. He appeared to be tall. His mustache and goatee were neatly trimmed. His nose was strong. His dark eyes were deep-set. His dark hair was curly and short with touches of gray. He wore an expensive dark suit with a white shirt and a blue silk tie. He was sipping a martini.

As soon as she was seated he spoke to the waitress. She took his order and brought Jordan a martini. Jordan picked it up and gestured with it at the man. He raised his glass and they touched rims. I ordered a beer. The bartender put down a dish of nuts. I ate some so as not to hurt his feelings.

Jordan and her companion gave some evidence that Doherty's fears were not groundless. They sat close together. She touched him often, putting a hand on his forearm, or on his shoulder.

Once, laughing, she leaned forward so that their foreheads touched. All his movements were languid, not as if he was tired, more as if he was happily relaxed about everything. And very pleased to be him.

They had two drinks. He paid the check. They got up and went out. I left too much money on the bar and went after them. They walked back to Concord College together. Got into a Honda Prelude in the parking lot and drove out. I was parked down Main Street a way. By the time I got to my car they were out of sight. So instead I went over the Longfellow Bridge and drove down to Milton.

It took about a half hour to get to Brant Island Road. I parked on the corner with a view of the house where Dennis and Jordan lived. It was a white garrison colonial, with green shutters. The lights were on. There was a Ford Crown Vic in the driveway. At ten after eleven Jordan pulled the Prelude into the driveway next to the Crown Vic. She got out, straightened her pants a little, fluffed her hair for a moment, then took her briefcase from the car, closed the car door, and walked carefully to the house.

4.

IT DOES SOUND kind of affair-y," Susan said.

"I saw them together," I said. "It's an affair. But it's not proof of an affair."

"I know," Susan said. "Will you say anything to the husband?"

"I don't think so," I said. "It would just be my opinion."

"You want to offer him certainty?"

"I think until I can prove it, he'll refuse to believe it," I said.

Susan nodded.

"Hard to know, sometimes, what's best," she said.

"How about the truth?" I said.

She smiled.

"That's often effective," she said.

We were sharing sweet-and-sour pork for supper at P. F. Chang's in Park Square. Unless you think that sharing means equal portions for both. In which case, I was having sweet-and-sour pork, and Susan was having a couple of bites.

"But I don't know," I said, "at this stage of things, if I would have wanted to know without certainty."

"You already had reason for suspicion," Susan said.

"I did, but I couldn't believe it."

"Why not?"

"I don't know," I said. "I don't know if I couldn't believe you'd do it, or I couldn't believe it could happen to me."

"Or wouldn't," Susan said.

"Same result," I said.

Susan isolated a small piece of pork on her plate, sliced it in half, and ate one of the halves.

"So I think I'll wait until I can prove it," I said.

Susan nodded.

"Are you planning to burst in on them with a video camera?" Susan said.

"Ugh!" I said.

"How about planting some sort of electronic device?"

"Ugh!"

She smiled.

"Are you sure you're cut out for this sort of work?" she said.

"Doherty needs to know," I said.

"Even though it will cause him pain," she said.

"He's in pain now," I said.

She nodded again, and ate the other half of the small piece of pork.

"And the pain of knowing is better than the pain of not knowing?" she said.

"Yes."

She nodded. She seemed to have very little to say about this. Usually she had a lot.

"Do you have a plan for proving it?"

"None," I said.

"So what are you going to do?"

"What I usually do," I said. "Plow along, try not to break things, see what develops."

"And if nothing does?" Susan said.

"I nudge it a little," I said.

"Yes," she said. "You certainly do."

5.

THIS TIME I duked the doorman at the Marriott a twenty to hold my car out front. Unfortunately Jordan Richmond and her male friend didn't go to the Marriott. They went down the street to a bar called the Kendall Tap. It was small, so I waited outside across the street for two hours and twenty minutes until they came out and walked back toward the college. Before we got there they stopped beside a silver Mercedes sedan parked at an expired meter. The man took a parking ticket off the windshield and folded it and put it in his pocket. Then he went around and opened the passenger door. Jordan got in. He closed the door, walked back around, got in the driver's side, and drove away. Foiled again. Mostly to make myself feel better, I wrote down the license plate number. Then I walked back to the Concord College parking lot.

Jordan Richmond's car was still parked there. That meant that her friend would need to bring her back. I went over to the Marriott and got my car from the doorman, and parked on the street near the Concord College parking lot. I was hungry. It was 7:13 on the dashboard clock. If Jordan kept to last night's schedule she wouldn't be picking her car up until about ten. I thought about a baked bean sandwich with mayo on anadama bread. I thought about corned beef hash with eggs. I thought about linguine with meatballs.

I wondered why I never thought about foie gras, or roast guinea hen, or duck with olives. I wondered if everyone was like that or was it because I was plebeian? Probably because I was plebeian. Maybe if you were more cultured you thought about Dover sole when you were hungry.

It had been raining in Boston much of the time since Labor Day, and it began again. I liked rain. I thought it was romantic. Susan didn't like it. It ruined her hair. I sometimes wondered how we could possibly be together. About the only thing we liked in common was us. Fortunately we liked us a lot.

There seemed little chance that linguine or Dover sole was forthcoming soon, so I watched the rain patterns on my windshield and thought about sex. Kendall Square at night is not lively. Now and then someone in rainwear would trudge past me. Occasionally a car, its wipers arcing slowly, would move along Broadway. The rest of the time it was just me, and the bright traffic lights reflected on the rain-shiny street.

At about ten of ten the silver Mercedes pulled up and parked next to the parking lot. The tall stranger got out and went around and opened the passenger door. Jordan Richmond got out wearing some sort of cowboy-looking rain hat. They held hands as they walked to her car. He waited while she unlocked the door. Then she swept her hat off and turned into him and they kissed good night. It was a long kiss, enough, probably, to straggle her hair, and it involved a lot of body English. Finally they broke and she got into the car, and then got back out again and they kissed again. Thank God the rain blurred it some. I tilted my head back and stretched my neck and looked for a long moment at the roof of the car. When I looked again she was getting into her car for the second time. This one took. He waited until her door was closed and her car was running before he walked back to his. She pulled out of the parking lot and headed for the Longfellow Bridge. I stayed put. When she was safely on her way, the tall stranger went west on Broadway, and I followed him.

He pulled into a garage on University Road, off Mt. Auburn Street. I lingered outside near the corner, where I could see both Mt. Auburn and University Road. He didn't reappear. The garage serviced a large condominium building under which it was located, and my guess was that the tall stranger lived there and had accessed it by an elevator in the garage. There was nothing more to see there. I decided to go home and reread my collection of Tijuana Bibles.

6.

THE SILVER MERCEDES was registered to Perry Alderson, whose address was in fact the Mt. Auburn Street building, unit 112, a condo above the garage where he'd parked. I got out my brown Harris tweed jacket, put it on over a black turtleneck, added a notebook and a camera, and drove over to Cambridge. I left my car with Richie the doorman at the Charles Hotel, and walked through the light rain over to Perry Alderson's building.

There was a woman at the concierge desk in the lobby. I smiled at her. A smile rich with warm sincerity.

"Hi," I said.

She was red-haired and pale-faced and, had she allowed any of it to show, she might have had a good body. But she was shrouded in one of those voluminous ankle-length dresses that seem to be part of the municipal code in Cambridge. So the condition of her body remained moot.

"Hello," she said.

"I'm writing a piece on urban living for *Metropolis* magazine," I said. "I was in Chicago last week, Near North, you know. And next week I'm in DC doing Georgetown."

"Really?" she said.

"Boston this week," I said. "Cambridge and the Back Bay."

"And you want to write about this building?"

"I sure do. It's a beauty."

"I'm afraid I can't let you bother the residents," she said.

"Oh, God no," I said. "Of course not. I don't need to. I was a guest here once, Mr. Perry Alderson, and I have pictures of his apartment and a lot of stuff I can use. But the fact-checkers are on my case. I remember I was on the first floor, number one-twelve, but I can't remember, was it the last one at the end of the corridor?"

"That's all?" she said.

"Absolutely," I said. "I have that, and I'm in business. Take a few exterior shots. Be out of your hair."

"Mr. Alderson is the last door on the left," she said.

I looked down the corridor past the elevators.

"On the left," I said. "I would have sworn it was at the end."

"Mr. Alderson is on the left, sir," she said firmly.

"What a memory," I said. "Some journalist. May I take your picture?"

She almost blushed.

"Photography is not permitted, sir, in the lobby, without permission of the condominium board."

"Of course," I said. "Of course. Can you do me one small favor?"

"Well, that would depend," she said. "Wouldn't it?"

"I'm going to sort of hedge this story a little, and I'm hoping this conversation could just be ours?"

"I am not a talker, sir," she said.

"I knew that," I said. "Beautiful yet mysterious."

This time she did blush. I winked at her debonairly, and walked away. The Compleat Journalist.

7.

WAITED NEAR the entrance to the lobby bar at the Marriott. Jordan and Perry were in place, having a drink. At about 7:40 they finished. Perry paid the bill while Jordan organized her things, and put the strap of her big purse over her shoulder. As they came out of the bar, I went in, jostled her slightly, dropped a small listening device into her bag, and said, "Excuse me."

She smiled absently and nodded and they kept going. As soon as they were gone, I turned and went out and ran through the rain to Hawk's Jaguar, which was idling across the street.

"Doorman had his car," Hawk said. "Silver Mercedes."

"Follow that car," I said.

Hawk looked at me as he put the car in gear.

"You being Boston Blackie?" he said.

"That would be you," I said.

"Lawzy," Hawk said. "Racial humor."

The silver Mercedes stopped by the Concord College parking lot. Jordan got out with her shoulder bag and went to her car. When she was in and the car was started, the Mercedes pulled away, and Jordan followed in her Honda Prelude.

"How come they splitting up?" Hawk said.

"Save him driving her back afterwards, maybe."

"Or maybe they know we on the case and they given up."

"We'll see," I said. "Radio tuned right?"

"Uh-huh."

I turned it on. There was a slightly muffled quality to the sound, but I could hear hip-hop being sung. I could also hear her windshield wipers. Pretty good.

"This isn't one of your stations," I said.

"Not my style," Hawk said. "She listening to the radio. "

The Prelude followed the Mercedes west on Broadway, which meant that she wasn't going home.

"Where you get the bug?" Hawk said.

"Voyeurs-R-Us," I said.

"Didn't know you was a spy tech guy."

"I consulted Emmett Sleeper," I said.

"Sleeper the Peeper," Hawk said. "Top drawer."

"He says this thing will listen at fifty feet and transmit an FM signal half a mile. Only problem would be background noise."

"They be doing what you think they doing," Hawk said, "background noise be the evidence."

I picked up a small tape recorder from the backseat and held it in my lap. I plugged the adapter into Hawk's cigarette lighter. Tested the thing for a minute, rewound it again, and shut it off.

"What she gonna think when she gets home later," Hawk said, "finds that thing in her bag?"

"If she knows what it is she'll know she's been caught."

"Think she'll stop seeing this guy?" Hawk said.

"No."

"Even though she figure the husband know?"

"He knows now," I said. "I had to guess, I'd say she wants him to know."

"So why don't she just tell him?"

"She also doesn't want him to know."

"And this a better way she can get even with him?" Hawk said.

"Maybe," I said. "If there's something to get even for."

Hawk grinned.

"There always be something to get even for," Hawk said.

The rain was heavy tonight, and there was a hard wind that made it seem even heavier. The Mercedes went into the garage beneath the condo, and the Prelude went in behind it.

"His place is in the back, this side of the building," I said.

"How you know?" Hawk said.

"Detective," I said.

"I keep forgetting," Hawk said.

Hawk parked near the back of the building.

In a moment the sound of the hip-hop stopped, then the wipers. The car door opened and closed. I pressed the record button on the tape recorder. I heard Jordan's voice, slightly muffled, but sufficient to understand.

"I can't wait to get naked," her voice said.

I could hear a man laugh.

"Do you think we're oversexed?" Jordan said.

Male laughter.

"Probably," the male voice said.

Footsteps.

"Isn't that good," Jordan's voice said.

Elevator doors. Elevator sound. Jordan giggled.

"What if someone opened the elevator door?" the man's voice said.

"We could say I was helping you look for your keys," Jordan said.

The male voice said, "I think we should wait until we're in my apartment."

"Damn," Jordan's voice said.

More giggling. Elevator doors. The giggling stopped. Footstep sounds. A door.

"A drink first?" the man said.

"Maybe a short one while I fluff up."

The bag bumped on the floor, a rustle of movement, then, faintly, a sound that might have been a shower. I was uneasy. I felt slightly short of breath. I could feel Hawk looking at me.

"Maybe we got enough," Hawk said.

I shook my head.

"Hear it through," I said.

Which we did. All of it. Sitting in the darkened car with the wind driving the hard rain straight in against the window. We listened to the sounds of obvious intimacy. At one point Jordan actually screamed. And giggled.

Once she said, "Perry, what are you doing to me?" in a little-girl voice.

Perry laughed. Otherwise he was quiet. Things culminated and then there was quiet.

After a time Jordan's voice said, "Oh my God."

Perry said, "Ever like this at home?"

"No," Jordan said. "Nothing."

I felt as if my soul were clenching like a fist. I was listening to something I had no right to hear. I thought about Doherty. Would I share this with him? Not unless I had to. I could probably convince him by playing the *I-can't-wait-to-get-naked* part. The stuff before she was noisily in bed with another man.

"We got plenty," Hawk said.

I nodded and shut off the tape. Hawk reached for the radio switch.

"Shall we have a drink while we talk about what you know?" Perry said.

Hawk's hand stopped. He looked at me.

"Postcoital?" he said to me.

"Let me get my body covered," Jordan's voice said.

"I like your body the way it is," Perry said. "Stay here. I'll get us a drink and we can talk in bed."

"Perfect," Jordan said. "I'll tell you what I've learned from Dennis."

I turned the tape recorder back on.

8.

WE LISTENED. Our street opened at the far end onto the river. Compressed by the high buildings on either side, the wet wind made the car tremble when it gusted. Inside it was just us and the two voices.

"Dennis says that the bureau knows that there is some sort of antigovernment activity associated with Concord," Jordan said. "But as far as I can tell it is no more interesting to them than half a dozen other groups."

"My name ever come up?" Perry said.

"Only in my dreams," Jordan said.

Hawk grunted.

The heavy rain flooded down the windshield, distorting what little we could see, making us seem alone in oceans of dark space, listening to disembodied words through the radio speaker.

"I hope you don't talk in your sleep," Perry said.

"Even if I did," Jordan said, "poor Dennis wouldn't make anything of it. He doesn't know what to make of me, for God's sake, or what to do with me. He has pulled his ignorance up around himself and hides."

"How do they know about Last Hope?" Perry said.

"Nothing that I know of."

"You ever mention it to him?"

"No, of course not. For obvious reasons."

"Of course," Perry said.

"According to Dennis, the bureau's attention is focused at the moment on a group called FFL. I don't know what the initials stand for."

"Freedom's Front Line," Perry said.

"Are they violent?" Jordan said.

"The philosophy is purgative," Perry said.

"By violence?"

"Yes."

There was silence, then Jordan said, "Sometimes it almost seems the only way."

"I know," Perry said.

"I wonder if I could do it?" Jordan said.

"Fight?"

"Kill," Jordan said, "for a cause I believed in."

"Fortunately you probably won't have to make that decision," Perry said.

"I don't know," she said. "This country. The way this country is going . . ."

"I know," Perry said.

He sounded very soothing.

"Does Dennis talk about the bureau's anti-terrorism operations?" Perry said.

"There's something called Operation Blue Squall," she said. "But I don't know much about it."

"It would help us in our mission," Perry said, "if we knew more."

"I know. I'll try. But Dennis and I don't talk so much anymore."

"Because of us?" Perry said. "He knows there's something going on?"

"I can't be here," she said, "with you, and home with him. He knows I'm not there."

"What else does he know?"

"He doesn't even know what he knows," Jordan said. "I told you he's got his head down like a man in a sandstorm."

"What if he decided to find out?" Perry said.

"He won't."

"He's an FBI agent," Perry said. "He has resources."

"Maybe," Jordan said. "But none that will help him here."

"I hope you're right."

"I'm right," Jordan said. "I've lived with him for twenty-five years. The poor bastard."

"You feel sorry for him?"

"He's so overmatched in this," she said.

"So what do you think you should do?" Perry said.

"Right now," Jordan said, "I think I should give you a blow job."

"That'll work," Perry said.

I reached over and shut off the radio.

"You don't want to listen to a BJ?" Hawk said.

"No."

"Might be some more clues," Hawk said.

"I got all the clues I can stand."

We were quiet. The wind and rain kept coming.

"She find that bug in her purse," Hawk said, "gonna matter more than we thought it would."

"I know."

"You working on a plan?" Hawk said.

"I am," I said.

9.

OW COME I got to mug her?" Hawk said.

"Sell the mugging," I said. "You're a big scary black guy. People expect to get mugged by big scary black guys."

"I too dignified-looking to be a mugger," Hawk said.

"It'll be dark," I said. "Besides, I don't want her to recognize me later."

"How about the guy? If he walks her to her car? What you want me to do with him?"

"After the evening he has spent, would you get up and get dressed and walk down to the garage?"

"Good point," Hawk said.

"And she's not going to raise a ruckus either," I said. "She's not supposed to be here."

"Okay," Hawk said.

Hawk pulled the car up to the corner and turned off the lights.

"Don't want her copping the plate numbers," he said.

Hawk turned the collar up on his leather trench coat and got out into the downpour. He walked down the street away from me and turned into the garage. I punched the radio on.

"Until tomorrow," Perry's voice was saying.

"Yes," Jordan said.

There was silence.

Then Jordan said, "I love you."

"I love you too, my friend," Perry said. "I love you very, very much."

Too many *very*s, I thought. Insincere. The door closed. She walked to the elevator. It went down. She got out. I could hear her heels on the concrete floor of the garage. Then I heard her stop.

"I'll take the bag," Hawk said.

"Don't hurt me," she said. "You can have the bag. I won't give you any trouble. Just don't hurt me."

"Car keys in the bag?"

"Yes. Take the car if you want."

I heard Hawk rummage in the bag. His hand an inch from the transmitter.

"You take the keys," he said.

I heard him walk away from her. In another moment he was out on the street. In another couple of moments he was in the car, the rain glistening on his shaven head. He plonked the bag in my lap, fastened his seat belt, and we drove away.

Then I shut off the radio, took the bug out, and switched it off. I put the bug and the tape recorder in a gym bag in the backseat.

"Easy," Hawk said.

"Thinking of taking it up?" I said. "Some sort of regular basis?"

I took Jordan's wallet out of her bag. There were two twenties, a driver's license, a Concord College ID, and some credit cards.

"Augment my income," Hawk said.

"You gave her back her car keys," I said.

"Gentleman Mugger," Hawk said.

There was a small emergency makeup kit in the bag, a small blue notebook, two ballpoint pens, an emery board, a packet of Kleenex, and a pair of reading glasses. The notebook was devoid of notes.

"Want to split the forty dollars?" I said.

"Split, hell," Hawk said. "I done all the mugging."

I handed him the two twenties.

"Fair's fair," I said.

10.

MAILED Jordan Richmond's wallet back to her, with an anonymous note saying I'd found it on the street. Then I called Doherty on his cell phone and said I needed to report, and he said he'd come to my office. He showed up ten minutes later wearing a camel-hair topcoat over a dark suit. He took the topcoat off when he came in and put it on Pearl's couch, which stood against the far wall to the right of the office door. Pearl wasn't visiting today, so the couch was empty.

"Whaddya got," he said.

His shirt was very white. His tie was striped red and blue. His face looked stiff.

"Your wife is having an affair," I said.

His face got stiffer.

"You got proof?" he said.

"Yes."

"Lemme see it."

"It's a tape recording," I said. "It'll be hard to hear."

"Play it," he said.

"You don't want to take my word?"

"Play the tape," he said.

I nodded.

"Okay," I said. "First some background. She's been seeing a man after work every night. She went to his apartment several nights. One night before she went I was able to slip a bug in her tote bag."

He sat motionless while I spoke. I had no way to know if he'd heard me.

"Play it," he said.

"There's a lot of silence and aimless noise on the tape," I said. "I edited it out."

He stared at me. I took the tape recorder out of my desk drawer and put it on the desktop and pressed the play button.

"I can't wait to get naked. . . . Do you think we're oversexed?"

I stopped the tape.

"Enough?" I said.

"Play it all," he said.

"You know already what you wanted to know," I said.

"I want to know everything."

I pressed the play button again.

"What if someone opened the elevator door? . . . We could say I was helping you look for your keys . . . A drink first? . . . Maybe a short one while I fluff up . . ." The bag bumped on the floor . . . a sound that

might have been a shower . . . The sound of intimacy . . . Jordan screamed . . . and giggled . . . *"What are you doing to me? . . . I think I should give you a blow job."*

I shut it off.

"That's all there is," I said.

Doherty was rigid. His face was flushed. He looked past me out the window. His eyes filled.

" 'I think I should give you a blow job,' " he said.

"Hard to hear," I said.

"You ever hear anything like that?"

"No."

"Then how the fuck do you know how hard it is?"

"I'm guessing," I said.

"Who is he?"

I expected the question. It was possible he'd go looking for Perry with a gun. It was possible he'd use the gun on himself. Or on his wife. I couldn't make those judgments for him. He had a right to know.

"Name's Perry Alderson," I said.

"How's she know him."

"I don't know," I said.

"What's he do?" Doherty said. "He work there?"

"I don't know."

There were things I suspected about Perry, but they didn't seem like things that Doherty had a right to know. At least until I knew.

"Find out," Doherty said.

I nodded.

"You going to be all right?" I said.

"I don't know."

He stood suddenly and walked past my desk and looked out my window.

"What are you going to do?" I said.

"I have no idea," Doherty said. "I have absolutely no idea what to do."

His voice had thickened. His shoulders began to shake. He was crying. Without another word he turned from my window and left my office.

I sat for a while after he left, looking at nothing, breathing deeply, trying to locate exactly what it was I was feeling.

11.

I T WAS ABOUT THREE in the afternoon. The rain had stopped, and the day was bright and not very warm when I walked down Cambridge Street to the Government Center Holiday Inn. I was meeting the special agent in charge of the Boston FBI office. His name was Epstein and he was at the bar with a Coke when I got there.

"That's tempting," I said.

"The Coke?" Epstein said. "Bureau is really pissy about having the SAC drunk during business hours."

I ordered a scotch and soda. Epstein turned his glass slowly on the bar in front of him.

"Sure," Epstein said. "Rub my nose in it."

"What do you know about an organization called Last Hope?"

Epstein stared at me.

"What am I, Public Information?"

Epstein didn't look like too much. He was balding and kind of scrawny, and he wore round dark-rimmed glasses that looked sort of stark against his pale skin.

"The bureau have any interest in them?" I said.

My drink arrived.

"As far as I know, the bureau never heard of them."

"Which means you never heard of them," I said.

"Same thing," Epstein said. "But I'll check."

"How about a guy named Alderson?"

"Who he?" Epstein said.

"He appears to be the head of Last Hope."

"Again," Epstein said, "I'll check, but as far as I know, we don't know him or his outfit and we have no interest. Should we?"

He continued to turn his half-drunk glass of Coke slowly on the bar in front of him, using just the tips of his fingers, watching the procedure as if it were interesting.

"Don't know yet," I said.

I took a drink. Epstein looked up and watched me sadly as I drank.

"How about Operation Blue Squall?"

The glass kept turning. Epstein continued to look at me sadly.

"What about Blue Squall?" Epstein said.

"I understand it's an anti-terrorism project," I said. "Which is currently interested in an outfit called Freedom's Front Line."

Epstein stopped turning his glass and sat back in the high-backed bar stool.

"FFL," Epstein said. "You want to tell me how you know about this stuff?"

"I want to tell you some of it," I said.

"I may want all of it."

"Cross that when we come to it," I said.

Epstein nodded.

"I'm working on a divorce case," I said. "Husband thinks the wife is cheating on him, wants me to find out if she is."

"Exciting work," Epstein said.

"Right up there with investigating subversives like Dr. King."

"Okay," Epstein said. "Okay. We did do some work in Mississippi, too."

I nodded.

"So I find out that the husband's fears are justified, and for proof, I bug the love nest and listen to them."

The excitement of the turning Coke glass seemed to have waned for Epstein. His attention was on me with nearly physical force.

"The lover is Alderson," I said. "The husband appears to be one of your agents."

"Shit!" Epstein said. "Who?"

I shook my head.

Epstein was silent for a moment, then he took his cell phone off his belt and dialed a number.

"Shauna?" he said. "It's me. I've run into something and I won't be back in the office today . . . no, in the morning . . . tell him in the morning . . . thanks, babe."

He broke the connection and put the cell phone away. Then he signaled to the bartender and when she came pushed the Coke toward her.

"Take this away," he said. "Bring me an Absolut martini on the rocks with a twist."

We sat silently beside each other at the bar until the martini came. He looked at it for a moment, picked it up, and took a meaningful pull.

"Better?" I said.

"You have no idea," he said.

"I might," I said.

"I'm going to have to know who the agent is," Epstein said.

"He may be guilty of nothing but a bad marriage," I said.

"I have to know," Epstein said.

"Yes," I said. "You do. But I won't tell you until I know the deal."

"You can get jugged for contempt," Epstein said, "until you tell me."

"I know," I said.

"But you won't tell me anyway."

"No."

"Might put some pressure on the guy hired you," Epstein said.

"Might," I said.

"If he's a stand-up guy," Epstein said.

"He might be."

Epstein drank some more of his martini. He looked affectionately at the glass while he swallowed.

"I have worked with you a couple times," Epstein said, "and know you to be a big pain in my tuchis."

"Nice to be remembered," I said.

"You been a tough guy so long, you forgot how to be anything else."

"But sensitive," I said.

"My ass," Epstein said.

"Wow," I said. "Two languages."

Epstein finished his drink and gestured for another. The bartender looked at me. I nodded.

"What we got brewing here," Epstein said, "is a fucking impasse."

"We do," I said.

"Which is not going to do either one of us any good," Epstein said.

"True," I said.

Our drinks came. We both allowed them to sit untouched for a dignified moment. Then we both took a swallow.

"You got any thoughts on how to resolve it?" Epstein said.

"I do."

"Thought you might," Epstein said. "Keep in mind that counterterrorism is not grab-ass. One of my agents gets compromised, people may die and some of them may not deserve to."

"I know," I said.

"Your plan?" Epstein said.

"I'll find out," I said.

"What?"

"Everything, and I'll keep you informed on anything you need to know."

"And you decide what I need to know?"

"We'll collaborate on that," I said. "If I find that your agent is compromised, I'll give him to you."

"I agree to that and the bureau finds out, I'll be working the teller's window at a drive-in bank in Brighton."

"If you can make change," I said. "I was never good making change."

"When you say everything, do you include Blue Squall?"

"Not unless I bump into it," I said. "I'll investigate my client, his wife, and her lover."

"Perry Alderson," Epstein said.

I hadn't mentioned Alderson's first name.

"Yep."

"Last Hope," Epstein said.

"Yep."

"We'll look into it from that end," Epstein said.

"Maybe we'll meet in the middle," I said.

"We fuck this up," Epstein said, "and I go down in flames."

I shrugged.

"Think of it as a blaze of glory," I said.

"And if I do," Epstein said, "I'll take you with me."

"No pain, no gain," I said.

12.

I SAT AT the counter and sipped a scotch and soda, tall glass, a lot of ice, to support the two I'd had with Epstein. I liked to drink alone in the quiet room. This was widely held to be the hallmark of a problem drinker, but since I rarely drank too much, and since I could drink or not drink as circumstance dictated, I was able to relax about it, and have a couple of drinks alone, and have a good time.

Susan was in New York overnight for a conference and Pearl was visiting me. I had fed her when I got home, and taken her out, and now she was on her couch looking at me without censure. Pearl II was a solid brown German shorthaired pointer like her predecessor. Thanks to the magic of selective breeding, she was, in fact, very much like Pearl I, which was sort of the idea. A way to manage mortality a little. She loved Susan and me, and running, and food, and maybe Hawk, but it was never clear to me in what order. I raised my glass to her.

"Here's looking at you, yellow eyes," I said.

She thumped her short tail a couple of times.

"Epstein is not being entirely open," I said.

Pearl settled her head on the arm of the couch so that she could look at me without the effort of raising her head. Her eyes weren't really yellow, they were more golden, or topaz. But *Here's looking at you, topaz eyes* didn't have the same ring.

"He knew who Perry Alderson was." I took a drink. "And I bet he knows what Last Hope is."

Pearl II was almost five now. She had been with us long enough so that the transition had become nearly seamless. It was difficult to remember which Pearl had done what with us.

"And he sure as hell is going to look into both of them."

My drink was gone. I got up and made another one.

"Epstein's also going to nose around quietly and see if he can find out which agent is having problems with his wife."

I wondered why I didn't just dump it all in Epstein's lap. The bureau has its ups and downs, but Epstein was an up. And he had resources. Far more than I did.

"The poor bastard," I said.

Pearl gazed at me blankly.

"Doherty," I said.

Pearl lapped her muzzle once.

"Adultery happens," I said. "Hell, it happened to me."

I drank again.

"'Cept we weren't exactly married, so I guess technically it wasn't adultery."

It sounded to me as if maybe *technically* came out as *tenichly*. Fortunately Pearl didn't know the difference, and had she known, she wouldn't have cared anyway.

"But that was a long time ago," I said.

Pearl seemed to have lost interest. She shifted onto her back with her feet up and her head lolling over the edge of the couch.

"Even before Pearl the First," I said.

I got up and found a lamb shank in the meat keeper. I put it in a casserole dish with some carrots and onions and some small red potatoes. I sprinkled in some oregano and a splash of white wine, put the cover on, and slid it into the oven at 350. I set the timer for an hour, made myself another drink, and took it with me while I walked to my front window and looked down at Marlborough Street. It was empty. But not very dark. The streetlights had an effect and it was still early enough in the evening for the lights to be on in front windows and that brightened things as well. I liked the look of it, of the light spilling domestically from front windows while people ate late supper together and maybe shared a bottle of wine.

"She'll be home tomorrow," I said to Pearl.

The recent winds had shaken some of the leaves loose from the trees. The trees weren't bare yet. But they were in the process. There was an occasional wind still stirring and, now and then, it scattered some of the leaves along the sidewalk. It made me think of a poem. I looked back at Pearl, whose position was such that her ample jowls had fallen away from her rather significant teeth.

It had been a long time ago, more than twenty years, since Susan had gone off for a time. In the long run the episode had been good for us both. And we had healed stronger at the break. That was then, this is now. That was us, not Mr. and Mrs. Doherty.

"A thing is what it is, and not something else," I said aloud in the rich silence of my apartment.

I looked out at Marlborough Street for a while. At the wedge of the Public Garden I could see across Arlington Street. I sipped my drink. I rarely got drunk. But *rarely* is not *never*. Then I looked back at Pearl, who was now asleep.

"Or maybe it is Margaret that I mourn for," I said to her.

13.

MET IVES in a place called Cornwall's in Kenmore Square, where they had approximately four hundred billion kinds of beer on draft. I couldn't try them all, so I settled on my favorite, Blue Moon Belgian White Ale. Ives had something dark and strong-smelling which I couldn't identify.

"Well, Lochinvar," Ives said. "What maiden are we rescuing this time?"

"I'm interested in what you know about an organization called Last Hope."

"Our mandate does not include domestic matters," Ives said. "I've told you and told you."

"How do you know it's domestic?" I said.

"Ah," Ives said and smiled. "You remain clever, don't you."

"As best I can," I said. "When I'm not drunk."

"Always a difficult condition," Ives said and drank some of his ugly beer.

Ives was tall and angular, slightly stooped, with a wiry neck. He was wearing one of those checked soft hats like Bear Bryant used to wear, and a Burberry trench coat, with a plaid bow tie showing.

"Off the record," I said.

"Of course," Ives said. "When you and I talk there is no record."

I nodded.

"Last Hope," I said.

"And you'll keep me in the loop," Ives said.

"Yes."

Ives leaned a little closer to me, and his voice dropped. I had to listen hard.

"Last Hope is an odd organization, and very difficult to characterize," Ives said. "It is run by a gentleman named Perry Alderson. No one is quite convinced that it is his real name. But we know him by no other."

"What does it do?" I said.

"We're not sure," Ives said softly. "It appears to be a kind of brokerage for terrorism."

"Brokerage?"

"They put bombers in touch with bomb makers, assassins in touch with people seeking an assassination. They collect information and sell it to people who need it."

"How big is the organization?"

"Don't know. It's not possible from where we are to figure out who is a member and who is temporarily with them, being brokered, so to speak."

"More than Alderson?"

"Probably. But he's the visible one. There are a few people who seem primarily to be protectors, and there may be more important people in the shadows behind him."

"Funding?"

"We don't know if it's funded," Ives said, "and if so by whom. We surmise that they are paid for their brokerage efforts."

The rain was back and Kenmore Square was brilliant with it in the late-afternoon traffic rush. There was a lot of commotion at the entrance as umbrellas were opened or closed, raincoats were donned or removed.

"Is it operative on any kind of scale?" I said.

"Nationally, we think, though the base camp seems to be here."

"They have a relationship with any foreign power?"

"Several," Ives said. "We think. Probably in the Middle East, and Central Asia, possibly in South America, maybe some parts of Africa."

"That's as specific as you can get?"

"Alderson has visited those places. People from those places have visited him."

"That's it? What kind of spy operation are you running."

Ives almost winced visibly at the word *spy*. I knew he would. It's why I used it.

"We have a great many irons to heat in the fire," he said sort of stiffly. "It's a big fire. In fact, we have a lot of big fires. We can't spare many people on one small blaze."

I nodded.

"Alderson any kind of ladies' man?" I said.

"There are women around him. We don't know what his relationship with them might be."

"Know the names of any of them?"

"No."

The wind shifted and the rain blew hard against the plate-glass window that looked out at the crisscross of Beacon and Commonwealth which created Kenmore Square. Ives and I both watched it rain for a little while.

"Is there anyone who might be with him more than others?" I said.

"The lady in the tower?" Ives said.

"Not exactly," I said.

"What exactly?" Ives said.

I told him some of it, leaving out the identities of Jordan and Dennis. Making no reference to the FBI. Without the FBI it wasn't a very compelling story. But I was stuck with it. Ives drank some of his beer thoughtfully, and put the glass down carefully.

"Ah, young Lochinvar," Ives said. "You are a lying sonova bitch."

"I have told you nothing that isn't true," I said.

"And left out much that is," he said.

I smiled.

"Your profession has made you cynical," I said.

"As it should," Ives said. "As would yours, and yet you remain sentimental."

"What makes you think I'm driven by sentiment?"

"I know you, Lochinvar. Our first collaboration was over your young lady, I believe."

"Long time ago," I said.

"Indeed," Ives said. "I also know your word is good. I'm willing to let you run a tab, because you said you'd keep me in the loop, so sooner or later, I will be."

The bartender came down to see if we needed a refill. We didn't. I gave him a twenty and told him to keep the change. He did. When the bartender departed, I looked at Ives.

"Despite your appearance," I said, "and the fact that you talk funny, it is good now and then to be reminded that you're not just another jerk from Yale."

Ives smiled, as he stood and buttoned his trench coat.

"Dear boy," he said. "There are no jerks from Yale."

"Never?" I said.

Ives continued to smile.

"Well," he said. "Hardly ever."

14.

IT WAS THE beginning of November. The clocks had fallen back and it was starting to get dark at four in the afternoon. I stood on the Cambridge end of the Longfellow Bridge with Hawk and Vinnie Morris, and looked down at the dark water. The river here was more like a lake, widened and slowed by the dam a couple of blocks east.

"She might recognize you," I said to Hawk, "so Vinnie's going to take her. I'll take Alderson, and you pick up any third party that joins them."

"She won't recognize me," Hawk said.

"You all look alike in a dark garage?" I said.

"Uh-huh."

"Play it safe," I said. "Let Vinnie take her."

"What if they five or six third parties?" Hawk said.

"Your call."

He nodded.

Vinnie said, "You got a picture?"

I gave him one. Vinnie looked at it in the failing light. He was a medium-sized guy with very precise movements, like some sort of well-made intricate device. He was one of the two best shooters I'd ever seen. The other one being a guy from LA named Chollo. If they shot it out, I'd have bet on both of them.

"Any chance I can fuck her?" Vinnie said. "Never fucked a professor."

"Maybe later," I said.

Vinnie nodded. He looked thoughtful.

"Yeah," he said. "Maybe."

"Vinnie," Hawk said, "you gonna fit right into the liberal scene."

"Sure," Vinnie said.

"We'll pick her up at the college, out front," I said. "Her office hours end at four-thirty. She always comes out the same door and heads for the Marriott bar, or the Kendall Tap."

It was nearly dark when Jordan came out of Foss Hall and turned left toward the Kendall Tap. She joined Alderson and two guys and a woman in a large round booth. I sat at the bar near them. Vinnie sat at the opposite end where he could look at them. Hawk took a seat at the turn of the bar so he could keep his back to them. He'd have three people to follow when they broke up. I wondered how he'd decide.

The Tap was long. Interior walls of exposed brick. Tiffany lamps. A horseshoe bar, and three huge television sets playing without sound above the bar. There was a jukebox somewhere and it played most of the time. But since I thought Bill Haley and the Comets was the cutting edge of new music, I didn't hear much that I enjoyed.

Jordan had so far resisted the Cambridge professor look. Her clothes bespoke designer labels, and money. She wore them with thoughtful respect for how good her figure was. Alderson too was stylish. Tonight he was wearing a gray suit with a silver tie. The other woman wore an ankle-length flowered dress with clogs. The two men were in jeans and T-shirts under Polar Fleece jackets. One of them wore a Greek fisherman's cap. All three were younger than Jordan and Alderson.

Jordan made no effort to hide her affection for Alderson. She always had a hand on him. Rubbing his shoulder, patting his forearm, resting on his thigh. Alderson seemed barely to notice. It was obvious he didn't mind, but he showed no sign that he sought it either. It seemed as if he found it to be just part of the environment.

The other woman, if she had worn makeup and managed her hair better, might have been good-looking, if she stopped dressing like Molly Pitcher. It was clear that she was with the guy in the light blue jacket wearing the Greek fisherman's cap. That's how Hawk would decide. If she left with one of the guys, he'd follow them. Economy. Two birds for the price of one.

They were all drinking wine, except Alderson, who had something on the rocks, probably scotch, and was sipping it as if he wanted it to last. There was a lot of talk, and a lot of laughter, both of which were led by Jordan. Alderson seemed to enjoy it quietly. Shortly after seven, Jordan whispered something in Alderson's ear. He laughed. They stood, said good-bye, and left. Vinnie and I went after them. Hawk stayed with the remaining trio.

When the evening ended, I didn't know much more than I had before the evening started. Hawk told me that the woman in the long dress and the guy with the Greek fisherman's hat lived together in a second-floor apartment on Magazine Street in Cambridge. The names on the doorbell downstairs were Lyndon Holt and Sheila Schwartz. Vinnie told me that Jordan had gone straight home and stayed there.

"Not enough to crack the case," I said.

"You wanted us to crack it?" Hawk said.

"Be nice," I said.

"Shoulda said so before," Hawk said. "We thought you the detective."

"Hard to tell sometimes," I said. "Hawk, you stay on Alderson. Vinnie, stick with Jordan."

"What're you gonna do?" Vinnie said.

"I'm coordinating the investigation," I said.

"Try not to hyperventilate," Hawk said.

15.

JORDAN RICHMOND STRODE into my office right after nine a.m., her heels decisive on the oak floor. I was standing in my window bay drinking coffee and watching the career women hurrying to work along Berkeley Street. I turned when I heard her heels.

"You're Spenser," she said.

"Accept no other," I said.

"Don't be frivolous," she said. "Did you give those tapes to my husband?"

"Those which captured the sounds of your indiscretion?" I said.

"Don't be evasive," she said. "Of course those tapes."

"So he played them for you," I said.

"Yes. Did you make them?"

"I did," I said.

"You had no right to make them," she said.

"But I did," I said.

"And I may very well sue you," she said.

"Let me know what you decide," I said. "Would you like some coffee?"

"Don't you realize you may have destroyed my marriage?" she said.

"Shoot the messenger," I said.

"What? . . . Oh, you're saying I destroyed my marriage."

"I'd guess that depends to some extent on how you and your husband feel about monogamy," I said.

She looked good: blue suit with a skirt that ended above the knee. High black boots, a white turtle. Her makeup was good, her hair was in place, everything was swell, except that she looked tired. Given the length and vigor of her evenings, I might have looked a little tired, too.

"I want those tapes," she said.

"Nope."

"All of them," she said.

"Nope."

"How much do you want?"

I was still in my window bay. I looked down and saw Vinnie across the street. He too was observing the career women, while he waited for Jordan to come out. He looked up at my window. He had probably guessed where she was. He saw me. I saw him. Neither of us had any reaction, but I smiled to myself.

"I asked, how much money do you want?" she said.

"I won't sell them," I said.

"They're mine. You have invaded my privacy. I am determined to retrieve it."

"Might be sort of like retrieving virginity," I said.

"I want those tapes," she said.

"Why?" I said. "The cat's already out of the bag."

She sat suddenly in one of my client chairs. It was as if her backside had collapsed and taken the rest of her with it.

"I have to have them," she said.

"What else is on there you don't want known?" I said.

She began, quite forcefully, to cry.

"Is this good?" she said as she cried. "You like to see women cry?"

I didn't see any light at the end of that tunnel so I didn't say anything.

"It will ruin my life if you won't give them to me."

I shook my head.

"Stop it," I said. "You're embarrassing us both to no avail. If you want to talk about how your life will be ruined, maybe I can help you avoid it. But this is pointless."

"What," she said. "If it's not money, what? Sex? Is it sex? You can have sex if you want. Just give me the tapes."

"I'm certainly flattered," I said. "But no thanks."

"I do want to have sex with you," she said around the sobbing. "You're very desirable. Really, just give me the tapes, honestly, I would enjoy it."

"Stop it," I said.

"I'm very good. I know how to do everything."

"Stop it," I said again. Harder.

She took a deep breath and I was afraid for a moment that she was going to run down a catalogue of what she was good at. But she didn't. She stared at me with the tears running down her face and her chest heaving and let the breath out without speaking, and dropped her head. We sat for a minute. Then she stood up abruptly and headed for the door, with her head still down.

"I'll get them," she said without looking up. "Goddamn you, I will get them."

She left without closing the door. I stood in the window looking down until I saw her come out of the building. Across the street Vinnie took a look at her and glanced up at me. I turned my palms up and shrugged. Vinnie strolled after her as she headed up Boylston Street on foot.

I walked over and closed my office door and walked back to my desk and sat. I wondered if she knew how to do anything I didn't know how to do? The options weren't limitless. Maybe Susan would have a thought.

16.

I T WAS A bright morning. Early November and people were strolling past my corner as if it were still summer. I was reading the paper, celebrating the return of *Calvin and Hobbes* with two donuts and an extra coffee. Doherty came into the office.

"I threw her out," he said.

"Jordan," I said.

"Yeah, I threw her out of the fucking house."

"You hurt her?" I said.

"No, I mean I didn't touch her. I told her to get out and she went."

"She say where she was going?"

"No," he said. "It's over. Gimme your final bill."

"She take anything with her?"

"I let her pack a suitcase. Gimme your bill."

"You don't want me to find Alderson?"

"Fuck him," he said. "It's over. I don't care where he is."

"It would be a bad idea," I said, "to go after him."

Doherty's face was pale except for redness around his eyes. He nodded.

"I know," he said.

"There's life after death," I said.

"I know that, too," Doherty said. "I'm going to survive this; I won't kill him."

"Good."

"I'll always regret it, though," Doherty said.

"Not killing him?"

"Yeah."

"Nice to think about," I said, "on cold winter evenings."

"Yeah."

"You might want to talk with someone," I said.

"A shrink?"

"Might help."

"I don't need it," he said.

"Got a guy if you do," I said. "Guy named Dix, specializes sort of in cops."

"I'm not a cop," he said.

"FBI," I said. "Close enough."

"How'd you know that?"

"I'm a trained investigator," I said. "Plus your wife said so on the tape."

"I didn't hear that."

"Cutting-room floor," I said.

"Maybe I should hear the whole thing," he said.

"Maybe you should move on from it all," I said.

He was quiet for a moment. Then he nodded slowly.

"Yeah," he said. "Maybe I should."

I wrote out Dix's address and phone number on a piece of notepaper and gave it to him. He took it and folded it up and stuck it in his shirt pocket without looking at it.

"Anybody at the bureau know about this?" he said.

"No."

I knew the question would come and I had already decided on my answer. By now Epstein might have figured something out. If he had, there was nothing Doherty could do about it. If he hadn't, there was no point in him worrying about it.

"Good," he said. "Doesn't help, you know, it gets around that there's trouble at home."

I nodded. Doherty stood. I waited.

Finally he said, "We didn't start off so good, but you been pretty decent with all this."

"Thanks," I said. "I'll send you the bill."

He nodded, and hesitated another moment, then turned and left.

17.

DO YOU THINK he'll be all right?" Susan said.

I was pouring some scotch into a tall glass filled with ice. It took concentration to get it just at the right level.

"Doherty?" I said. "Yeah, I think so."

I added soda precisely to the rim of the glass and stirred the ice around with the handle of a spoon.

"He's an FBI agent," Susan said. "He carries a gun. He comes from a culture that puts some premium on machismo."

I took a sip of my scotch and soda. Perfect.

"He's pretty tough," I said. "He's willing to take the short-term pain for long-term gain."

"Meaning?"

"Meaning it would be a source of great pleasure for him to shoot Alderson dead," I said. "But it would probably ruin his life. And the satisfaction of remembering the shooting wouldn't be enough to compensate."

"Goodness," Susan said. "You've given this some thought."

"Yes," I said. "He'll move on."

It was a Friday night. Susan had just come upstairs from her last patient of the week. She was wearing one of her subdued shrink outfits, a dark suit with a white shirt. The kind of outfit that says, *It's about you, not about me.* She took the suit jacket off and hung it on the back of a chair. I smiled. She wouldn't look subdued in a flour sack. The best she could do was to barely avoid flamboyant.

"So it's over as far as you're concerned," she said.

"The case?"

"Yes."

She got a bottle of Riesling from the refrigerator and poured some for herself, and came and sat at the other end of the couch from me, with her legs tucked up under her.

"Not entirely," I said. "I'd like to know what Jordan and Alderson are doing, and whether the FBI has been compromised."

"Patriotism?" she said.

"I don't want to see this guy lose his job, too," I said.

"Because of his wife."

"Because he told things he shouldn't have told to a woman he thought loved him," I said.

"They'd fire him for that?"

"You bet," I said.

"Maybe she did love him," Susan said.

"Funny way to show it," I said.

"Maybe she was doing what she had to," Susan said.

"Maybe we all are, all the time," I said. "But if you really believe that, there's not much point to either of our jobs."

"Yes," she said. "Even if it's an act of self-deception, it's one we need."

I smiled.

"So we aren't exactly free," I said, "even to believe in free will?"

She stuck her tongue out at me.

"Oh, pooh," she said. "It's an academic game. We both believe in individual responsibility, and we both know it."

I smiled at her.

"And if we didn't before, we do now," I said.

Pearl had been asleep in the big leather wing chair across from us. She rose quite suddenly and came and stared at us.

"Has Timmy fallen down a well?" I said.

"It's suppertime," Susan said. "She wants Daddy to feed her."

"I would have said she was looking at you," I said.

"Did you go to Harvard?" Susan said.

"No."

"Did I?"

"Yes," I said.

"She wants her daddy to feed her."

"Sure," I said, "now that you've explained it."

I got up and went to the kitchen and gave her a bowlful of dog food and came back to the couch. Pearl ate noisily. Susan looked at me over her wineglass. She had big eyes, which she made up artfully.

"I hope you don't get mired in Doherty's issues," she said.

"I hope I don't get mired in anything," I said.

"It wouldn't be too hard to do with Doherty," she said.

Pearl finished her supper and came in and looked at us again. I got up and gave her a cookie for dessert. While I was up I got myself a second drink and brought it back to the couch.

"Because of what happened to us twenty years ago?" I said.

"What do you think?" Susan said.

Pearl came in from the kitchen and wedged herself between us on the couch and put her head on Susan's thigh.

"I've thought of it," I said. "It resonates."

"Want to talk about it?" Susan said.

"Sex might make it better," I said.

"You think sex makes everything better," Susan said.

"Uh-huh."

"Maybe you're right," Susan said. "Let's see."

18.

WAS IN the shower the next morning when Susan came in wearing La Perla lingerie.

"Vinnie's on the phone," she said.

I got out and toweled off a little.

"You want to stand and admire my glistening body while I take the call?" I said.

"No," she said and handed me the cordless phone and departed.

I said, "Yeah?"

Vinnie began without preamble.

"I follow the professor the other night to Alderson's place. She don't meet him for drinks. She goes straight there. I see Hawk there, scouting Alderson. Professor's got a suitcase. She goes in. I wait. Hour later she comes out. Still got the suitcase. She gets in her car. Drives about a hundred feet to the hotel next door. Parks in the garage. Checks in to the hotel. I wait awhile. She don't come out, so I go home. Hawk's still there. This morning I'm there when she comes out of the hotel. No suitcase. Gets in her car, drives to the college. Parks in the lot, gets out and starts for her building. Guy walks up behind her and shoots her in the back of the head. I put one in him. Go over and check. She's dead. He's dead. I get back in the car and watch for a little while. Nothing happens. No one comes out for a look. I don't hear no sirens. So I screw. I'm in the parking lot at Dunkin' Donuts down near Fresh Pond Circle."

I was quiet for a minute. Pearl wandered in to admire my glistening body. I patted her head while I thought.

"Any witnesses?" I said.

"No."

"Anybody looking out a window," I said, "maybe got your plate numbers?"

"Plates are bogus," Vinnie said. "I put on new ones before I called you."

"How long since the shooting?"

"Hour, probably," Vinnie said.

"Cops should be there," I said.

"Sooner or later," Vinnie said.

Pearl heard Susan moving around in the kitchen and hustled out of the bathroom to investigate. You could never be certain someone wouldn't give you a second breakfast.

"Recognize the shooter?" I said.

"No. Little guy. Five-six, five-seven, skinny. Dark hair cut short. Maroon sweatsuit. Cheap black running shoes."

"Don't be a fashion snob," I said.

"Don't matter anyway," Vinnie said. "He won't be using them."

"Okay," I said. "Eat a few donuts, drink some coffee. I'll get back to you."

I walked into the bedroom and sat on the bed. Susan had made it already. My gun lying on the bedside table looked very much out of place. I had dried off so that my body no longer glistened. Susan would have to settle for quiet beauty. I dialed Hawk's cell phone.

"What's up with Alderson?" I said.

"In his hole," Hawk said. "Been there since yesterday afternoon."

"People in or out?" I said.

"Not that I can tell."

"Somebody aced Jordan Richmond," I said.

"And?" Hawk said.

"Vinnie killed him."

"That'd be Vinnie," Hawk said.

I told him what I knew.

"Vinnie got a whole assortment of license plates," Hawk said. He laughed softly. "Clip-ons."

"Good to be prepared," I said.

"'Specially being Vinnie," Hawk said. "Cops going to connect you to this."

"I know."

Susan came into the room fully dressed and saw me still naked sitting on the bed. She covered her eyes.

"Ick," she said.

"You got an alibi?" Hawk said.

"I do," I said. "I was seeing my shrink."

19.

EPSTEIN CAME NONDESCRIPTLY into my office and sat in a client chair.

"Coffee?" I said.

"Yes."

I took a clean coffee cup from my desk drawer and handed it to him and pointed at the coffeemaker on top of my file cabinet. Epstein got up and helped himself.

When he sat down again he said, "Three days ago the wife of one of my agents got shot to death in the parking lot of Concord College."

I nodded.

"She used her maiden name, Jordan Richmond," Epstein said.

"In her circles I think they say *birth name*," I said.

"In her circles there aren't any maidens," Epstein said. "Another man, whom we can't identify, was killed with her, and Ms. Richmond's husband, Dennis Doherty, is missing."

I nodded.

"Thing is," Epstein said, "Ms. Richmond was killed with a Russian-made nine-millimeter which was found at the scene. The guy who was killed with her was done by a nine too, but not the same one."

I nodded.

"The Russian piece had the dead guy's fingerprints on it," Epstein said. "Powder residue on his right hand and forearm."

"So he shot her," I said.

"Probably."

"Who shot him?" I said.

"Don't know."

"And you can't ID the guy shot her?"

"Nope. No fingerprints in the system. No DNA in the system. Nothing on him. No driver's license. Didn't have a wallet. Didn't have any money. No car. No subway tokens."

"So how'd he get there?"

"Exactly," Epstein said.

"And how was he going to get away?"

"We speculate somebody delivered him and was waiting to pick him up when something went wrong. So the pickup scooted."

"Maybe he was the other shooter," I said.

"Guy aces Ms. Richmond and his partner aces him?"

"They were pretty careful that he have no identity," I said.

"We talked to everyone at the college who knew Ms. Richmond," Epstein said.

"Good thinking," I said.

"Seems she was keeping company with a guy named Alderson."

"Whoops," I said.

Epstein sipped his coffee and waited.

"Okay," I said. "Dennis Doherty hired me to find out if his wife was having an affair. She was. I told him."

"And he believed you," Epstein said.

"I had audiotapes of her and Alderson in, ah, *flagrante*."

"And he believed those."

"Yes."

Epstein grimaced.

"He listened?"

"Yes."

"Hard to hear," Epstein said.

"It was," I said.

"How did he react?"

"Like he'd been gutted, wanted to kill the guy."

"Not his wife?"

"No," I said. "He wouldn't kill his wife."

"Because?"

"He loved her."

"Lotta guys kill the woman that cheated on them," Epstein said.

"Not if they love them," I said.

Epstein looked at me, thoughtfully. Then he shook his head slowly.

"You actually believe that," he said.

"You don't kill someone you love," I said.

Epstein shrugged.

"Besides," I said. "Looks like you know who killed the woman."

"Doesn't mean Doherty didn't contract him."

"You think he did?"

"No," Epstein said. "Doherty was much too straight ahead. He was going to kill her he'd have done it himself."

I nodded.

"He had it under control last time I saw him," I said. "Said he wouldn't kill the guy either. Said he wouldn't let them flush his life."

"You think it was real?" Epstein said.

"We talked about it. He'll go to his grave wishing he'd put a couple into Alderson. But he'll know he was right not to."

Epstein gave me the long thoughtful look again, but he didn't comment.

Instead, he said, "They been having trouble for long?"

"I don't think so," I said. "Or maybe they had, but he refused to know it."

"So this would have come as a shock."

"Yeah."

"I gather you weren't tailing the broad any longer," Epstein said.

78

"No," I said, "I wasn't."

"You give Dennis the audiotape you played for him?" Epstein said.

"Yes."

"I don't remember it being inventoried," he said.

"You've tossed his place?"

"We've looked around," Epstein said. "We'll look again."

He got up and went to the file cabinet and got more coffee.

"Got any thoughts on whether he got compromised?" Epstein said.

"Nothing I didn't tell you at the Holiday Inn bar," I said.

"Anything about Alderson?" Epstein said.

I shook my head.

"Wasn't that interested in Alderson," I said. "I was hired to be interested in Jordan Richmond."

"You got any idea why she got killed?" Epstein said.

"No."

"Or who the killer was?"

"No."

"Or if somebody hired him?"

I shook my head just for a change of pace. It was as if Epstein was running down a checklist in his head.

"And if somebody did hire him," Epstein said, "who that might be?"

"Nope."

"Or where Dennis Doherty is?"

"Not a clue," I said.

"Sadly," Epstein said, "me either."

20.

I T HAD BEEN an odd fall. It rained every day for about six weeks, and now, two weeks before Thanksgiving, it was sunny, and temperate enough to sit on a bench in the Public Garden and have lunch. Some of the trees were leafless, but many of them still had a full complement. Yellow mostly, with some red and now and then some green.

"You should drop Alderson for the moment," I said to Hawk. "Epstein will be all over him."

Hawk nodded. He ate a small plastic forkful of curried chicken salad from his plastic takeout dish.

"For the moment?" he said.

"We might want to revisit him later," I said. "Depends on developments."

"Why not just leave it be?" Vinnie said. "You got nobody paying you."

Vinnie had a meatball sub which, because his movements were so precise, he was able to eat without getting any on his shirt. I could get chewing gum on my shirt.

"Spenser don't leave things be," Hawk said. "You know that."

"Why don't he?" Vinnie said.

"I don't know," Hawk said.

He looked at me.

"Why don't you?" he said.

"Something buried in my deep past," I said.

"What?" Vinnie said.

"That mean he don't know either," Hawk said. "But I promise you he ain't gonna let this alone."

"You know that," Vinnie said.

"Ah do," Hawk said.

"How you know?"

"He gonna think she died on his watch."

"He wasn't even there," Vinnie said. "Fuck, if you want to talk about that, she died on my watch."

"That bother you?" Hawk said.

"Bother? No." Vinnie was puzzled. "I wasn't protecting her . . . I nailed the guy clipped her."

"He's different than us," Hawk said.

"Could you guys discuss me on your own time?"

"'Course not," Hawk said.

I laughed.

"The guy you clipped," I said to Vinnie. "How did he get there?"

"No car?" Vinnie said.

"No car," I said. "No car keys. FBI and the Cambridge cops went through every car parked in the lot or on the street. Identified all the owners. None of them was your guy."

Vinnie shrugged and took another precise drip-free bite of his sandwich.

"Subway."

"No wallet. No money. No tokens. No pass. Even if he used a token to get there. How does he leave?"

Vinnie chewed thoughtfully for a moment.

When he was through he said, "You don't want to hit somebody like that and have nowhere to go."

Hawk nodded.

"Crowded area, maybe," Vinnie said. "You pop the mark and mingle with the crowd. But not here. Nobody's gonna hit somebody in the bright morning and plan to stroll away in Kendall Square."

"Don't like to depend on no subway either," Hawk said.

"Be a driver," Vinnie said.

"See anybody?"

"No," Vinnie said. "Wasn't looking for anybody."

"Untraceable piece," Hawk said. "No ID, no money, no means of transportation."

"Had to have a driver," Vinnie said. "When he saw the shooter go down, driver took off."

"Somebody going to a lot of trouble, keep him a secret," Hawk said. "Case he got caught."

"How could they be sure he wouldn't talk, if he got caught?" I said.

None of us knew.

"So you going to chase this thing?" Vinnie said.

"Probably," I said.

"You know why?" Vinnie said.

"Because I can't sing and dance," I said.

21.

EPSTEIN CALLED ME from his car.

"Doherty's dead," Epstein said. "Want to ride along?"

I did.

There were a couple of cruisers, and a couple of unmarked cars and a coroner's wagon parked near the water behind UMass, Boston. Doherty was not recognizable, a sodden something wedged in among some boulders. Frank Belson was there.

"Been in the water awhile," he said. "Hard to say where he went in."

"Cause of death?" Epstein said.

"Have to wait till they open him up," Belson said. "Body's been banging against rocks and things."

"Any estimate when?"

Belson shook his head.

"Same thing," he said. "You know what they're like in the water. When did he go missing?"

Epstein told him.

"Consistent," Belson said. "Coulda died then."

"No sign of his car?" Epstein said.

"Not yet," Belson said. "Makes me think he didn't go in here."

"We can check the currents," Epstein said.

"Sure," Belson said.

Epstein nodded. He walked over and stood looking down at the remains. I saw no need to.

"Currents are kind of unreliable around here," I said.

"That's for sure," Belson said. "But we check them anyway."

"That may be the definition of police work," I said.

"Philosophical," Belson said. "You in this?"

"He was having trouble with his wife," I said. "He hired me to look into it."

"And?"

"She was cheating on him," I said.

"You tell him?"

"Yes."

"Where is she?" Belson said.

"She was shot to death," I said. "Couple of days ago."

"In Cambridge?"

"Yes."

"That don't simplify anything," Belson said.

"No."

"So what are you doing here now?"

"Epstein invited me," I said. "Interested party."

The wind off the ocean was hard. Belson had his hat clamped down against it. Everyone was hunched a little.

"Aren't you always?" Belson said. "If I remember, the wife was shot by someone who got shot himself."

"Yeah," I said. "Too bad."

"Been nice and neat if the other guy hadn't done it. Doherty shoots his cheating wife and then goes and jumps off a bridge someplace."

"Clear two cases," I said.

"No such luck," Belson said. "Coroner doesn't come up with a neat explanation, we're going to have the bureau up our ass for the foreseeable future."

"You can work with Epstein," I said.

"Sure, they leave it with him," Belson said. "But they bring some of those guys up from DC . . ."

"I know," I said.

"You know anything I don't know?" Belson said.

"Christ, where do I start?" I said.

"About this case?" Belson said. "You holding anything back."

"No."

"You always hold something back," Belson said.

"Don't generalize," I said.

Belson nodded. Epstein still stood, motionless, looking at the remains of Dennis Doherty, while the photographers photographed and the measurers measured and the routine went on around him.

Two more unmarked cars arrived and men got out wearing dark jackets that said FBI on them.

"Help is on the way," I said.

"Oh fuck," Belson said.

22.

HAWK AND I were working out at the Harbor Health
Club. Probably out of some loyalty to his own past, and
because he liked Hawk and me, Henry Cimoli kept a small
boxing area in the club that was otherwise full of gleaming
machinery and chrome-coated weights. Hawk was hitting the
little double-end jeeter bag with his left hand and I was doing
combinations on the heavy bag. The more repetitious the
exercise, the more you are likely to coast. I concentrated on
punching through the bag. Hawk seemed to hit the jeeter bag
without any effort or thought, except he hit it square every time
and it danced rhythmically. He shifted hands without breaking
the rhythm.

"You know what be bothering me?" he said.

"The question of intelligent design?" I said.

"I already know that," Hawk said. "What I'm thinking is that if Vinnie ain't there to drill the mystery shooter, that everybody be assuming that her husband shot her and killed himself."

"Uh-huh."

"So maybe somebody set it up that way," Hawk said.

"And Vinnie showed up and ruined it," I said.

Hawk began to hit the bag alternately with both hands. The rhythm was uninterrupted. I paused and watched. It was Hawk in essence. Like everything he did, it seemed effortless, as if he were thinking of something else. And yet the perfectly focused energy seemed to explode through the bag.

"Not their fault," Hawk said. "They had no reason to think he'd be there."

I went back to working my combinations on the heavy bag.

"That theory might lead one to speculate," I said between punches, "that Doherty was murdered too."

"Would," Hawk said.

"And one might wonder who was responsible."

"Alderson seem to be the honky in the woodpile," Hawk said.

"She went straight there after her husband kicked her out," I said.

"She in there 'bout an hour," Hawk said.

"Plenty of time to tell him what happened," I said.

Hawk shifted his feet a little and went back to hitting the small bag with his left hand.

"So why didn't she spend the night?" I said.

"Maybe Alderson only like to fuck part-time," Hawk said.

"It would explain why she went to the hotel," I said.

"Lotta rejection," Hawk said. "And the next day, she dead, and her husband missing."

"Probably dead by then too," I said.

"She know 'bout you?" Hawk said.

"Yes."

I put a final flourish of combinations on the heavy bag.

"Epstein tells me they haven't found that tape among Doherty's possessions," I said.

"Doherty got no reason to get rid of it," Hawk said.

"No. Be useful in a divorce proceeding."

"Maybe he knew there wouldn't be none," Hawk said.

"You mean he hired someone to kill her?"

"People do."

"Not him," I said. "Not his style. He might have shot her in a rage and then put the gun in his mouth. But he wouldn't hire some guy with no ID to do it, and then drown himself later."

"Okay," Hawk said. "Maybe Alderson don't want people to know he been fooling around with Jordan."

"Killing two people to cover it up seems extreme," I said.

"Maybe he don't want people knowing other things," Hawk said.

"If he does and he stole the tape he'll be disappointed," I said. "I edited it down to just the lovey-dovey stuff."

"But you still got the original."

"Yes, I do," I said.

"Anybody know that?" Hawk said.

"Not yet," I said.

"So maybe they think they got all there is," Hawk said.

"Maybe."

"On the other hand," Hawk said, "they know somebody made the tape."

"Yep."

"So they ain't free and clear yet," Hawk said.

"Nope."

"Unless Jordan told them 'bout you."

"My guess is that she didn't," I said. "She was pretty desperate to get them back, more than she should have been, since her husband had already heard them."

"She worried about Alderson," Hawk said.

"Maybe."

"So maybe she don't tell him," Hawk said.

"Maybe."

"Doherty could have told them 'bout you before he died?"

"He was FBI," I said. "They may have thought he did it himself."

Hawk finished up with an elegant flurry of punches, and stepped away from the jeeter bag and looked at me. He nodded.

"They don't know," Hawk said.

"That's my guess."

"They knew," Hawk said, "they would have made a run at you already."

I nodded.

"So we're probably under their radar," I said.

"There you go with that *we* again," Hawk said.

"I leave you out and you get sullen," I said.

"I always sullen," Hawk said. "You thinking about letting them know you got the tape."

"It's an option," I said. "Let's see what develops."

"You could just give the tape to Epstein," Hawk said. "Then there'd be no reason for them to come after you."

"And there'd be no way to smoke them out," I said.

"You won't give Epstein the tape," Hawk said.

I shrugged.

"It's our only hole card. Otherwise these people have no reason to show themselves."

"They might get Alderson arrested," Hawk said.

"You heard them," I said. "Did he ever say anything that would get him jail time?"

"No."

"But as long as there's a tape and he wants it," I said.

"If he wants it," I said.

"Mr. and Mrs. Doherty died for a reason," I said. "And the tape's missing."

"'Less you buy it's suicide," Hawk said.

"You?" I said.

"No," Hawk said.

"So it's a working hypothesis," I said.

"I got another one," Hawk said.

"Which is?"

"They killed these people on your time," Hawk said.

"You could think of it that way."

"You could and you do," Hawk said. "I know you a long time."

"I've tried to be a good role model," I said.

"So you want the one gets them be you," Hawk said. "Not Epstein."

"At least I want first position," I said.

Hawk smiled widely.

"'Course you do," he said.

23.

EPSTEIN STOPPED BY my office in the late morning and gave me a big brown envelope.

"Copy of Alderson's file," he said.

"What makes you think I'm interested," I said.

"I know about you," he said.

"Anything classified?" I said.

"I work for a very large government bureaucracy," he said. "My fucking dick is probably classified."

"And should be," I said. "You got anything new on Doherty or his wife?"

"Water in his lungs. He was alive when he went in."

"And conscious?" I said.

"No way to know," Epstein said. "No bullets in him, no discernible wounds on the body. But it's been banged around on the rocks and chewed on by sea creatures. Nothing is certain."

"Time of death?"

"Approximate with his wife, give or take twelve hours," Epstein said.

"Tidal analysis?" I said.

Epstein smiled.

"Body could have gone in most places north of the Cape," he said.

"It was saltwater in his lungs," I said.

"Yes."

"Wearing his gun?" I said.

"Nope."

"Holster?"

Epstein smiled again.

"Nope," he said. "Nobody appears to have disarmed him. Gun and holster were in the top drawer of a bureau in his bedroom."

"Did it appear to be her bedroom, too?" I said.

"Yes."

"How was he dressed?" I said.

"Shirt, pants, shoes," Epstein said. "Wallet in his hip pocket. He wasn't wearing his suit coat or tie."

"Sounds like they took him at home."

"Which," Epstein said, "leads me to wonder where she was."

I nodded.

"You got any idea?"

"No," I said.

"I was married once, twice actually, and I remember some of it, and one of our female agents went through the house too, and we agreed that there wasn't enough makeup in the bathroom. Like she packed some and left."

"After he heard the tape," I said. "It would figure."

"So where'd she go?"

"Ask around at the college?"

"Nobody knows."

"Hotel?" I said.

"We're running that now," Epstein said. "Just thought you might save us a little time."

I shrugged.

"Sorry," I said.

Epstein sat quietly looking at me. Outside my window it was dark, with a lot of wind which drove short occasional bursts of rain against the glass.

"I talked with Martin Quirk about you," he said. "Known you a lot longer than I have."

"He's always admired me," I said.

"Sure," Epstein said. "He told me you get sort of flighty upon occasion."

"His admiration sometimes shades into jealousy," I said.

"We agreed that you sometimes operate under the illusion that you're Sir Lancelot."

"Explains why my strength is as the strength of ten," I said.

"That was Galahad," Epstein said.

"Wow, a literate bureaucrat."

"We also agreed that you were pretty good at this work and could go places and do things that cops are barred from," Epstein said.

"Fewer rules," I said.

"Mostly none, according to Quirk."

I shrugged.

"And we agreed that you usually came out on the right side in the end," Epstein said.

"When possible," I said.

"At the end of this," Epstein said, "you better be on the right side, which is to say, mine."

"Do what I can," I said.

"You better," Epstein said. "You get the full force and credit of the U.S. government on your ass . . . we'll win that one."

"Eeek," I said.

24.

IT WOULD HAVE been helpful if Vinnie hadn't shot the mystery man," Susan said.

I was driving, Susan beside me. It was dark. The wipers were moving gently. It embodied most of what I wanted in life, alone with Susan, going someplace, protected from the rain.

"It would be helpful if the tooth fairy came by," I said, "and left a note under my pillow explaining everything."

"I guess it was just Vinnie being Vinnie," Susan said.

"Yes," I said.

"It wouldn't occur to him that the gunman might be a valuable witness."

"It wouldn't," I said.

"And if it did?" Susan said.

"He wouldn't care," I said.

"Some nice friends," Susan said.

"I'm not sure Vinnie is a friend, exactly," I said. "But if I need him he shows up. He's not afraid of anything. He keeps his word. And he's a really good shooter."

I was in Kendall Square, looking for a parking spot close to the college. Susan would hate walking in the rain. Unlike myself.

"Who seems to be without regard," Susan said, "for any of the rules."

"He has some rules," I said.

"Like Hawk," Susan said.

I spotted an unoccupied hydrant across the street from Concord College.

"Some," I said. "He's not as smart as Hawk."

"Most people aren't."

"And he doesn't have Hawk's, what, joy?" I said.

Susan laughed.

"Oddly, *joy* is about right for Hawk," she said.

I let the traffic pass, and U-turned back toward my hydrant.

"It's almost as if we were talking about you," she said. "Which is kind of frightening."

"I have more rules," I said.

"I know."

"And I have you."

"Yes," she said. "You do."

I parallel-parked so adroitly that I was looking for applause. Susan had no reaction. She'd expected it. That was, after all, a kind of applause. We got out and headed across the street.

Susan had an umbrella. She offered me shelter under it. I declined, of course.

"This lecture," Susan said from under her umbrella. "It's by the man that Jordan whatsis was having an affair with?"

"Richmond," I said. "Yes. Epstein gave me the FBI file on Alderson, or at least as much of it as Epstein felt I should see."

"That's cynical," Susan said.

"You bet," I said. "According to the file, Alderson is a visiting professor at Concord, and part of his deal is to give two public lectures per academic year."

"And we're going to assess him?" Susan said.

"Got to start somewhere," I said.

"And you brought me along to help with the assessment?" Susan said.

"Yes."

"Not because it was going to be so boring you couldn't stand to do it alone?"

"Boy," I said, "you shrinks!"

We went into the college and found our way to the lecture hall. We sat in the last row. I put my feet on the back of the chair in front of me. No one else was within three rows of us. Susan smiled.

"Childhood habits persist," Susan said.

"I was always a little rebellious in school," I said.

"I'm shocked," Susan said. "Shocked, I tell you."

It was a big lecture hall, and could probably hold more than one hundred people. There were maybe thirty of us scattered around the room. A professor in an ill-fitting corduroy jacket came out onto the stage and introduced Alderson.

"My, my," Susan said when Alderson came onto the stage. "Handsome."

"If you like that look," I said.

"What look do you like?" Susan said.

"Thuggish," I said.

Susan smiled.

"Yes," she said. "I like that too."

After the lecture, some of the audience gathered around Alderson at the lectern. They were almost all women. Alderson was animated and charming with them.

"Recruiting a replacement?" I said to Susan.

"Women like him," Susan said.

We left, and, with the rain still coming pleasantly, we drove out to Arlington and had a late supper at a restaurant called Flora.

"Whaddya think?" I said.

"He's a graceful performer," she said. "Speaks well. Doesn't say much that's new and informative."

"The federal government is fascist, his organization is the place of last refuge for freedom-loving Americans," I said. "That's not new?"

"I don't admire this current government either," Susan said.

"Who does?" I said.

"Possibly eleven people somewhere back in the hills," Susan said. "But I remain unconvinced that Last Hope is the answer."

"What'd you think of him?" I said. "As him."

"We didn't see him," Susan said. "We saw his public persona. All we know is that he's capable of assuming that persona."

"On the tapes he was in his seduction persona," I said.

Susan sipped her martini.

"Did it resemble his public one?" she said.

"Less oratorical," I said.

"What does the FBI file say?"

I drank some scotch.

"Last Hope advertises itself as helping people in trouble with the government," I said. "According to the Feds, they claim to counsel the victims of government oppression on how to fight back and to provide access to lawyers, investigators, and CPAs."

"And do they do that?"

"Feds don't seem to think they do much of it."

"How many people in the organization."

"Feds don't know."

"Who finances them," Susan said.

"Feds don't know."

"Shouldn't they know more than they seem to?"

"They don't think Last Hope amounts to much," I said. "Or at least they didn't, until one of their agents got killed."

"And you?" Susan said. "You think they amount to much?"

"I don't know if they're in a position to bring our government to its knees," I said. "But I think Alderson killed two people."

"And you want him to answer for it," Susan said.

"I do," I said.

"You barely knew these people," Susan said.

"I knew them enough," I said.

The waiter brought salmon for Susan, and gnocchi for me. I had another scotch.

"And you withheld information," Susan said, "that might prove useful to the police and the FBI."

"For the moment," I said.

"Because you want to catch him yourself," Susan said.

"Yes."

She nodded.

"That's not unlike you," Susan said. "In any case."

I nodded.

"But you seem unusually intense about this one," she said.

"I'm an intense guy," I said.

"That's just it," she said. "You're not, at least not so it shows."

We were quiet for a moment. Susan waited.

"You think I identify with Doherty?" I said.

"Maybe," Susan said.

"Because you were with another man once?"

"There are parallels," Susan said.

"It was a long time ago," I said.

"That's right," Susan said.

25.

I AM CAPABLE of patience, but I don't enjoy it. And I had
been standing by, open-shuttered and passive, for about
as long as I could stand. I figured that Epstein probably had
Alderson's office bugged by now, and maybe his home. Being a
professional detective, I had already detected that Alderson's
duties at Concord, aside from the two public lectures, appeared
to be a three-hour graduate seminar called "An Alternative to
Tyranny," on Wednesday afternoons.

I hung around outside the seminar room until class ended.
The ten or twelve students, mostly female, gathered around
Alderson, talking excitedly with him. I waited. Alderson looked
at his watch and shook his head, and the students came out
and dispersed except for one woman, who looked to be in her

forties. She continued to talk animatedly with Alderson for a couple of minutes before he patted her hand and nodded and indicated his watch.

She took the hand he had patted her with and held it in both of hers for a moment. Then she let go and he stood and they came out together. She was maybe forty-five, with blond high-lights. She dressed well for a student, even an old one. She wore a wedding ring. And she was as shapely as Jordan had been. I wondered if her husband was privy to government secrets.

"Tonight?" she said.

"Won't be like any night," Alderson said and smiled.

The woman's face flushed. She giggled. She made a gesture as if she was going to take his hand, thought better of it, and touched his cheek briefly before she turned and headed down the hall.

Alderson headed down the corridor toward his office. I walked with him. He looked at me sidelong for a moment, decided he didn't know me, and strode on.

"Professor Alderson," I said.

He turned his head this time to look at me.

"Yes?"

"I have some audiotapes," I said, "that I think you should hear."

"Audiotapes?"

I gave him my card.

"Come see me," I said.

"What kind of audiotapes?"

"They're personal in nature," I said.

"Excuse me?"

"Jordan Richmond," I said.

"Jordan Richmond," he said.

"And you," I said.

He stopped and looked at me without any expression.

"Original recording."

His look didn't waver. His expression didn't change. It was as if somewhere inside there a valve had clicked shut.

"Come see me," I said again and walked away. "Bring cash."

When I got to the elevator he was still standing expressionless looking after me. No affect. If I weren't so valiant it would have been a little unsettling.

26.

THE NEXT MORNING, I got to my office early. The door
seemed intact. No sign of jimmying. No hint that anyone
had worked on the lock. There was no point in Alderson rush-
ing this. I probably hadn't told anyone, if I was looking for
cash. And if they just popped me first chance they got, they
might not find the tapes and they'd be right where they had
been before they popped me, so the sensible thing was for
Alderson to play along.

I took my gun out and held it at my side while I unlocked
the door and pushed it open. Nothing stirred. I waited. Nothing. I raised my gun and followed it into the room in a crouch.
The room was empty.

I left my office door open, and put my gun back on my hip, and made coffee. I sat at my desk and opened the right-hand top drawer, where I kept a stainless-steel Smith & Wesson .357 Magnum. There were six rounds in the cylinder. If seven guys showed up, I could throw the gun at the last one. I took the little tape recorder from my middle drawer and put it on my desk near my left hand. Then I opened the paper.

I was reading today's *Calvin and Hobbes.* Get it while it lasts. I liked the idea of rerunning stuff. Today *Calvin and Hobbes,* maybe someday *Alley Oop?* I had no fully developed plan for this venture. I had simply gotten tired of waiting and decided to poke a stick in the hive. I was being careful, but until Alderson could account for the tape, he probably wouldn't be dangerous. He might eventually decide that the best approach was simply to make me tell him what I knew. But that wouldn't come until he knew more than he knew now. For all he knew now, I was bait, and when he made a run at me a thousand FBI agents would jump out of the woodwork and say booga booga.

I read *Calvin and Hobbes,* and *Tank McNamara,* and *Arlo and Janis.* I was studying *Doonesbury* when Alderson came into my office alone. He closed the office door behind him and came to the desk carrying my business card in his left hand.

"Mr. Spenser," he said.

I folded the paper and put it down.

"Mr. Alderson."

He was wearing a gray Harris tweed jacket with a black turtleneck sweater and tan corduroy pants. A long red scarf was draped around his neck. I thought the scarf made him look like a horse's ass, but he seemed pleased with it. He was looking at me closely. Probably wondering why I didn't have a scarf. Then he tucked my card in his breast pocket and slowly looked around the room, at each wall, the floor and the ceiling. When he was through he studied my desk from where he stood. If he saw the gun in the open drawer, he didn't react. He sat down.

"Are you an agent of the United States government?" he said.

"No."

"Of any government?"

"No."

"Are you taping, or in any way recording, this conversation?" he said.

"No."

"What is the purpose of this meeting?" he said.

"I'm hoping to blackmail you," I said.

He tipped his head back, as if stretching the front of his neck, and held it that way for a moment. Then he lowered his head and allowed me to see that his face had no expression.

"That's rather bold," he said.

I smiled modestly. He waited. I sat. A silence ensued.

After a time, Alderson said, "Upon what basis are you planning to blackmail me?"

"I have an audiotape of you," I said. "Before, during, and after sexual congress with the recently deceased wife of a recently deceased FBI agent."

"Sexual congress is neither illegal nor rare," Alderson said.

"But the postcoital chitchat suggests that you may be involved in, ah, antigovernment activity."

"Who wouldn't oppose this government?" Alderson said.

"Matter of degree and method," I said.

Alderson gave me his blank dignified stare again, while he thought about things.

"Posit, as an hypothesis," Alderson said after a time, "that such a tape existed, how would I know you had it?"

With my left hand, I pushed the play button on the tape recorder.

"Shall we have a drink while we talk about what you know?" Alderson's voice said.

"Let me get my body covered," Jordan's voice said.

"I like your body the way it is," Perry said. *"Stay here. I'll get us a drink and we can talk in bed."*

"Perfect," Jordan said. *"I'll tell you what I've learned from Dennis."*

I shut off the recorder. Alderson pursed his lips slightly.

"Posit a second hypothesis," he said after a while. "That it was actually my voice on that tape, and that I wanted to acquire it, how much would it cost me?"

"Fifty thousand dollars," I said.

"What is to prevent someone from simply taking the tape from you?" Alderson said.

"Me," I said.

"You fancy yourself a tough guy?" Alderson said.

"Known fact," I said.

"And should one pay your price, how would one know one wasn't getting one copy of many?"

"One would not know," I said.

Alderson pursed his lips some more.

"You are arrogant," he said.

"Confident," I said.

Alderson mulled for a time.

"May I have time to consider this?" he said.

"Sure," I said. "Week from today, in the afternoon, I turn everything I got over to the special agent in charge, Boston office, FBI."

Alderson stood and looked down at me for a while with his eyes empty. Then he turned and left without speaking again.

27.

A N HOUR AFTER Alderson left, Epstein arrived.

"Alderson came to visit you," he said.

"He did."

"You made contact with him at the college yesterday," Epstein said. "And this morning he was here for about forty minutes."

"Your guys are pretty good," I said. "I didn't make them yesterday, and I was looking for them."

"We have our moments," Epstein said. "What's the story?"

"Off the record," I said.

"Off what record?" Epstein said. "You been watching television again. I didn't send a couple agents down to bring you in. I came here alone. In your office."

"I need your word," I said, "that we'll do it my way."

"No," Epstein said.

"Don't equivocate," I said.

"I can't give you my word blind," Epstein said. "I can't let you decide what's bureau business. Maybe I never could, but the rules have changed since nine-eleven."

I nodded. Epstein didn't say anything. I didn't say anything. We had gotten to the bridge we were going to cross when we got to it. And we both knew it. The muffled sound of traffic drifted up from Boylston Street. The sound of someone in high heels walking briskly came from the corridor outside my office.

"You asked me to trust you," Epstein said. "I can't do that. But what I can do is ask you to trust me."

I waited.

"Bureau business comes first," Epstein said. "That stipulated, I'll cut you as much slack as I can."

My office refrigerator cycled on quietly. Susan had decided I needed a refrigerator. It was a small one, next to the file cabinet. I kept milk in it, for coffee, and beer, for emergencies.

I opened my middle drawer and took out the tape recorder. I had rewound it to the beginning when Alderson left. Now I had only to punch the play button. Which I did. Epstein listened to the whole tape without saying anything.

When it was through he said, "Got a dupe?"

"Yes."

"Then I'll take that one," Epstein said.

I took the tape out of the recorder and handed it to him.

"Okay," Epstein said. "Talk to me."

I got us each some coffee, sat in my chair, put my feet up, and took a sip.

"I edited that tape down to the stuff Doherty had to hear to know she was cheating," I said.

"Why not play the whole thing?"

"He was going to have enough trouble hearing her cheat," I said. "I didn't want to make him sit through it all."

"And?" Epstein said.

"The next day she came here and begged me for the tape."

"So Doherty confronted her."

"Yes," I said.

"Played her the tape."

"I assume so."

"That must have been pretty," Epstein said. "So why'd she want it?"

"Wondered the same thing," I said. "She offered money. She offered sex. A combination of both. Whatever I wanted. She said if she didn't get the tapes it would ruin her life."

"Doherty know there was more on the tape than you gave him?" Epstein said.

"Yes."

"So she probably remembered that when they weren't talking blow jobs," Epstein said, "they were saying things that might draw attention to Alderson."

"I would guess," I said. "The day she came to see me, that evening she went to Alderson's condo with an overnight bag. She was in there maybe an hour and came out with the bag and checked into the hotel next door."

"She probably told him about the tapes," Epstein said.

"Probably."

Epstein drank a little of his coffee.

"And," he said, "she probably expected to move in with him now that her husband had kicked her out."

"Probably."

"And he said no."

"And they had a fight," I said. "And he gave her the boot."

Epstein got up, carrying his coffee, and began to walk around my office.

"She may not have told him about you," Epstein said.

"If she had," I said, "someone would have come after me."

"True," Epstein said. "And no one has."

"Once he got mad," I said, "she probably didn't want him to know that it was even worse than he thought."

"Dennis was FBI," Epstein said. "He'd know how. Alderson probably thought Dennis did the bugging."

"Yes."

"And the next morning after she told him this she was killed, and that same day, probably, her husband was killed."

"Sounds like Alderson," I said. "Doesn't it?"

Epstein was nodding as he walked.

"And when they searched his house and found the tape they thought they'd got it all?"

"She probably minimized the damage when she told him about the tape," I said.

"Seems a lot of trouble," Epstein said, "kill two people just to avoid being mentioned in a divorce proceeding."

"I guess he valued his privacy."

"You have a tail on the woman the day she was killed?" Epstein said.

"Yes."

"And it was your guy plugged the shooter."

"Yes."

Epstein walked past my desk into the little bay behind me, and looked down at the street and sipped his coffee. Neither of us spoke.

Then Epstein said, "Lotta nice-looking women walk by here."

"They do?" I said.

Epstein turned from the window and smiled.

"So," he said. "You got a theory of the case?"

"I do," I said.

"How 'bout that," Epstein said.

"I think that Alderson believed that he could insulate himself from any investigation by killing the only two people who knew anything. Jordan, because they were lovers. Doherty, because he'd heard the tape."

"Uh-huh," Epstein said. "Except the tape Doherty heard didn't have anything actually incriminating, unless we still prosecute for adultery."

"But Alderson didn't know that," I said. "Until he listened, by which time both Jordan Richmond and Dennis Doherty were dead."

Epstein nodded slowly, paused to drink some coffee, and nodded some more.

"So he tries to make it look like Doherty killed her when he learned of the affair," Epstein said. "And then, crazed with grief, he killed himself."

"But would the cops know of the affair?"

"We learned that she and Alderson were an item when we began investigating her death," Epstein said. "Lotta people knew."

"And," I said, "when you got to him he could say, *I'm sorry it turned out this way, but we are, after all, men of the world.*"

"But your guy tailing Jordan ruins it by putting one into the shooter's head. Nice shot, or a lucky one, hit him under the right eye."

"It wasn't luck," I said. "Too bad, though. If he hadn't been so good, the guy might not be dead and we might have an ID."

Epstein finished his coffee.

"Too bad," Epstein said.

"You knew who Alderson was before I ever came to see you," I said.

"He was a person of interest," Epstein said. "But pretty low priority."

"And his organization?" I said.

Epstein shrugged.

"Like you told us everything," he said.

"You started it," I said.

Epstein grinned.

"You got a plan?" he said.

"I want to bring him down," I said. "For the murders."

"And your FBI? He killed one of my agents. You want me to stand around and reload for you?"

"You get him for subversion or whatever you were looking at him for in the first place," I said.

"And if we overlap?"

"We'll adjust," I said.

"A race?" Epstein said.

"First one to bust him wins?" I said.

"He gets busted everybody wins," Epstein said. "I don't care who gets the credit."

"J. Edgar must be doing ring-around-the-rosy in his grave," I said.

28.

A ND HE DIDN'T ASK who shot the mystery assassin?"
Susan said.

"No."

"Well, that's some sort of vote of confidence, isn't it," she
said.

"He knows I wouldn't tell him."

"And he wants your help," Susan said.

"I can do things that are illegal for him."

"And you," she said.

"Sometimes," I said.

"But he can do things you can't," Susan said.

"He has resources I lack."

"So you avoid the minefields," Susan said. "And you both know that you're doing it, and you know why, and you don't say anything."

"We both want the guy that killed Doherty," I said.

We were at my place, I was making supper. She was at my kitchen counter, on the living room side. Pearl had claimed the couch, which she managed to occupy more fully than one would think possible for a seventy-five-pound dog.

"It's about Doherty," Susan said.

"Man was murdered," I said.

"His wife was murdered too," Susan said.

I mixed bread crumbs and pignolia nuts with a little olive oil, and began to toast them in a fry pan on low.

"Doherty was one of Epstein's," I said. "Makes it kind of personal."

"And you?" Susan said.

"Guy's going along doing his job, living his life, and his wife takes up with another guy, and it breaks his heart, and then gets him killed," I said. "That needs to be evened off a little."

I took the fry pan off the fire and emptied the toasted crumbs and pignolias into a bowl. I had a large pot of water boiling on the stove. I put some whole-wheat linguine in it and set my timer.

"But she doesn't need evening off? Because she caused the trouble in the first place."

"Alderson's responsible for both," I said. "We get him, we even everything off."

"You don't hold her responsible?"

"I don't know enough," I said. "Maybe Doherty drove her to it."

Susan nodded. She was sipping a glass of sauvignon blanc.

"Happens," she said.

After the pasta had cooked for three minutes I added slices of yellow squash and zucchini.

"You think I'm overidentifying with Doherty because of what happened to us all that time ago?" I said.

Susan smiled.

"Happens," she said.

"It didn't get me killed," I said.

"But people died," Susan said.

I nodded. I had a tall scotch and soda working and I drank some of it.

"Hawk thinks I'm identifying."

"He's spoken of it?"

"Not really," I said. "But it's what he thinks."

"And he's probably worried about it for the same reason I am," Susan said.

"Which is?"

"That you don't have enough distance on it," Susan said. "And it will get you killed."

"What I do entails a certain amount of that," I said. "We both know it. And we both move on. Nobody's killed me yet."

"You've set yourself up with Alderson," Susan said.

"He won't try to kill me. He doesn't know where the tape is."

"If he doesn't do something," Susan said, "your trap won't work."

"He'll do something," I said.

"What?"

"I don't know. When I boxed I was a counterpunch."

"So readiness is all," Susan said.

"Yes."

We were quiet for a moment.

"He might try to use you as leverage on me," I said.

"I need to do my work," Susan said. "I can't go somewhere and hide."

"We'll protect you," I said.

"I know."

"Hawk mostly," I said. "I don't want to draw them to you."

"Hawk will do," she said.

"He often does," I said. "I'm sorry this impinges on you."

She smiled at me.

"It's happened before," she said. "Goes with the job description."

"Which is?"

"Main Squeeze," she said. "And what about the matter of identifying with Doherty?"

The timer sounded. I poured the pasta and vegetables into a colander and let them drain for a moment.

"I know about the time you were with another man," I said. "And I know we're together now."

Susan nodded.

NOW *and* THEN

I put the pasta and vegetables in a bowl, added the toasted
crumbs, pignolias, and some grated cheese. I tossed it all with a
splash of olive oil. Susan watched me silently. I stopped tossing
the pasta and put the spoons down and looked at her. She put
her hand on top of mine where it rested on the counter.

"That's all I need to know," I said.

29.

H<small>E GONNA FIND OUT</small> who you are," Hawk said, "by now."

"Probably," I said.

"So he gonna figure out that you might be baiting him."

"But he can't be sure. Not all of us are equally honest," I said.

"He might find out that you are," Hawk said.

"Either way," I said, "he's going to have to do something."

"He could disappear," Hawk said. "Start over someplace else. New identity. Not so hard to do, you know a couple people."

"Feds are all over him," I said. "I doubt that he'll disappear."

"Feds ain't that good," Hawk said.

"Epstein is," I said. "And this is one of their own."

Hawk shrugged. We were in his car, parked on Linnaean Street across from Susan's home.

"You afraid he'll make a run at Susan?" Hawk said.

"If he's learned enough he'll know it's the only thing he can blackmail me back with. He can't come straight at me because he doesn't know where the tape is."

"You thinking 'bout reinforcements?" Hawk said. "Me and Vinnie gonna get spread pretty thin covering you ass and hers."

"I've made some calls," I said. "Until we get more feedback we'll all cover Susan's ass . . . so to speak."

"Lot better-looking than yours," Hawk said.

"I don't know," I said.

"Yeah, you do," Hawk said.

A bald guy, maybe forty-five, in a black jacket and a blue shirt, came out of Susan's front door and down the steps. I looked at my watch.

"Okay," I said. "Fifty minutes, right on schedule."

Five minutes later a young woman went up the stairs. She had on a gray jacket, unzipped, with a maroon sweater that ended four inches above her low-rider jeans.

"What you suppose her problem is?" Hawk said.

"Compulsive belly flasher," I said.

"Lotta that happening 'round here," Hawk said. "You call Tedy Sapp?"

"I did."

"Chollo?"

"Yep."

"And?"

"Sapp's out of the country. I talked to Mr. Del Rio. He said he could lend me either Chollo or Bobby Horse, but not both."

"Chollo," Hawk said.

"That's what I told him," I said.

"How 'bout the little dude from Vegas?" Hawk said.

"Bernard J. Fortunato," I said. "Couldn't locate him."

"Last time he helped us out, he got shot up," Hawk said.

"I know," I said. "Probably deserves a bye on this one."

"We got enough people anyway," Hawk said. "Hell, Chollo come aboard, and we got them outnumbered."

"You know it's not your fight," I said.

"Ain't Vinnie's fight," Hawk said, "or Chollo's either."

"That's right," I said.

Hawk smiled.

"Any fight will do," he said.

30.

ALDERSON CAME IN with a big red-haired guy who
looked like a tough hippie. Flannel shirt, work boots,
beard. Halfway to the desk, Alderson stopped and stared at
Chollo sitting on the couch.

"Who's this?" Alderson said.

"My friend," I said, "visiting from Los Angeles."

Chollo was slender and medium height, with a ponytail. He
looked with quiet amusement at the big red-haired guy.

"Why is he here?" Alderson said.

I pointed my chin at the big redhead.

"Protect me from the red menace," I said.

"Him?" the redhead said.

"*Sí,*" Chollo said.

"Oh, I'm scared," the redhead said.

"May I talk freely?" Alderson said.

"Absolutely," I said.

The redhead kept eyeing Chollo. Chollo paid him no further attention. In fact he seemed as if he might be about to nod off.

"I have your money," Alderson said.

"Good," I said. "I have your tape."

"Will this be the end of it?" Alderson said.

"You mean have I made a bunch of dupes," I said. "And is this the first of many payments?"

"Yes."

"I've kept a backup to protect myself," I said. "But I won't ask for more money."

"Not acceptable," Alderson said.

"Does this mean you're not going to give me the fifty large?" I said.

"Not unless I get everything," Alderson said.

"Okay," I said.

"Okay?"

"Give me the fifty, you get everything."

"How do I know I can trust you?" Alderson said.

"I'm paralyzed with fear of Big Red?"

"Mr. Spenser," Alderson said. "I do not respond well to frivolity."

"What a shame," I said.

"I will not be treated like this," Alderson said. "I will not pay you any money."

"And the tapes?" I said.

"There are many ways to get them," Alderson said. "Please remember that I attempted the most civilized way first."

"How could I forget," I said.

"This," Alderson said, "is not a whimsical matter."

"What kind of matter is it?" I said.

Big Red was eyeing Chollo as we talked. Red looked scornful. Chollo appeared to be thinking long thoughts about pleasant things.

"This government will use any means to silence me," Alderson said. "The tapes would give them a pretext."

"You don't even know what's on the tape," I said. "Except for the excerpt I played. What do you think they'll hear when they play it."

"You won't give the tape to them," Alderson said. "You will lose any chance at fifty thousand dollars and any other leverage with me that you might need."

"What other kind might I need?" I said.

"I will have those tapes one way or another," Alderson said.

Alderson turned on his heel and headed for the door. Big Red followed him. He stopped at the door and gave Chollo a long last look.

"Maybe I'll see you again," he said.

Chollo raised his head slightly and looked at Big Red through his half-closed eyes. Alderson was already in the hall.

"*Ay caramba,*" Chollo said.

Big Red went out without shutting the door behind him. Unmannerly.

"Well," I said. "That went well."

Chollo smiled.

"I'm here to protect you from that?" Chollo said.

"Give them a chance," I said.

"Why don't I go back to LA and send my little sister out?"

"They've killed a couple of people," I said. "One of them FBI."

"Anybody can kill anybody," Chollo said. "These people are amateurs."

I nodded.

"I know you won't go for it," Chollo said. "But I could spike both of them and be kicking back in Boyle Heights tomorrow."

"When's the last time you were in Boyle Heights?" I said. "Kicking back?"

Chollo grinned.

"1991," he said. "Been there since, but not kicking back."

"On business?" I said.

"For Mr. Del Rio," Chollo said. "How 'bout Hawk and Vinnie, they in this?"

"They're with Susan," I said.

"And I get you," Chollo said.

"Somebody had to," I said.

"So Alderson thinks there's a stalemate," Chollo said. "He's got your money and you've got his tapes and neither one of you can make a move without you losing the money or him losing the tapes."

"Yes," I said.

"So we sit around and await developments?" Chollo said.

"Maybe we'll snoop a little," I said.

31.

M Y PHONE RANG. It was Epstein.

"Alderson came to see you," he said.

"I told him I had the incriminating tapes, beyond what he got from Doherty's house."

"And?" Epstein said.

"I offered to sell them to him for fifty thousand. He came to negotiate."

"Who's the big red-haired guy?" Epstein said.

"Don't know," I said. "You photograph him?"

"Of course we photographed him," Epstein said. "We'll run him through the system."

"Show him to Belson, too," I said. "He remembers people that aren't in the system."

"You get the money?"

"No," I said. "I don't think he ever planned to pay it. He was just trying to get the lay of the land."

"You got some backup?"

"An adorable little Latin person," I said.

Chollo was drinking coffee.

"I'm not so little," he said.

"Well, I assume you hire good help," Epstein said.

"The best," I said.

Chollo nodded.

"He won't take a run at you until he knows where the tapes are," Epstein said.

"And he thinks I won't give you the tapes until I get my fifty thousand."

"A Mexican standoff," Epstein said.

"*Sí.*"

Chollo said, "You speak my language."

I grinned at him.

"Somebody talking to you?" Epstein said on the phone.

"My bodyguard," I said. "He likes to practice his English."

"Me too," Epstein said. "You think he's going to try for leverage on you?"

"Once he's sure greed won't do it," I said.

"You got Susan covered?" Epstein said.

"Yes."

"Hawk?" Epstein said.

"Yes," I said. "And Vinnie Morris."

"Don't recall Morris," Epstein said.

132

"He'll do," I said.

"So you don't need anything from me on that front."

"No."

"Well, stay on that," Epstein said. "Anyone who does any looking around knows that she's the breach in your wall."

"True," I said. "But she's also the wall."

"Whatever that means," Epstein said. "What now?"

"We'll see," I said.

32.

THE NEIGHBORHOOD ON Magazine Street, where Lyndon Holt lived with Sheila Schwartz, reeked of graduate student. The gray clapboard apartment building had once been a large single residence. The Holt/Schwartz apartment was a second-floor walk-up that overlooked somebody's two-car garage.

I rang the bell and waited. In a moment a woman's voice said, "Who is it?" over the intercom.

"Spenser," I said. "I called, from *Arsenal* magazine? I'm here with my photographer."

"Oh sure," the voice said. "Top of the stairs."

"*Arsenal*?" Chollo said.

I shrugged.

The intercom buzzed. I heard the door lock click and opened it. Chollo and I went into the little hallway and up the stairs. Chollo was wearing a camel-hair overcoat and carrying a camera bag over his shoulder. Sheila was standing in the open doorway. Low jeans, short T-shirt, showing a lot of stomach. If she was going to dress like that, I thought, she ought to do a lot of sit-ups. Lyndon stood behind her in the doorway. The full slacker: white T-shirt, multi-striped dress shirt, unbuttoned with the shirttails out. Jeans, hiking boots. Everything but the boots had obviously been home-laundered.

"Sheila says you're doing a piece on Perry?" Lyndon said.

"Yes," I said. "We thought it would make an interesting story the way events in the Middle East have, so to speak, reinvigorated the remnants of the counterculture."

"Remnants?" Lyndon said.

"The opposition had lowered its voice for a while there after Vietnam."

"They'd like you to think that," he said.

"Would you folks like some coffee?" Sheila said.

"That would be swell," I said. "You don't mind if my photographer takes some shots? You know, ambience shots, maybe some candids of you folks."

"No, that's fine," she said. "You don't mind, do you, Lyn?"

"I want to see the story before it's published," Lyndon said.

"That will be between you and my editor," I said. "Won't do any harm to have some pictures, however, in case we need to use them in the story."

"You mean we might end up in the magazine?" Sheila said.

"Definitely your names, parts of the interview. Pictures is up to the photo editor. We just send in the undeveloped film."

"I don't see any harm, Lyn," Sheila said.

He shrugged.

"Go ahead," he said. "But I'm not signing any photo release until I see what's in the story."

I nodded and looked at Chollo.

"Okay, Casey," I said. "Just get some informals while we talk."

"*Sí,*" Chollo said.

They both stared at him as Chollo took a big 35mm camera out of the bag and began focusing.

"He used to be a crime photographer," I said.

Chollo clicked off a couple of shots. They kept trying to smile into the camera as he moved around the room.

"Pay him no mind," I said. "They'll never use anything smiling into the lens."

They looked quickly away. I got out my notebook.

"So," I said. "How long have you known Perry Alderson?"

"Since we started grad school," Sheila said. "We took his seminar and it blew us away."

She looked at Lyndon. He nodded.

"Did you two know each other before you came here?" I said.

"No, we met in Perry's class," Sheila said.

"Where did you do your undergraduate work?" I said.

Chollo drifted around pretending to be Francesco Scavullo.

"Wisconsin," Sheila said.

"Berkeley," Lyndon said.

I wrote diligently in my notebook.

"And did you come here because of Professor Alderson?" I said.

"No," Sheila said. "At least I didn't. I hadn't heard of him until I got here."

"You?" I said to Lyndon.

He shook his head.

"Why did you come here?" I said.

"I liked the college," Lyndon said. "It had a reputation for, you know, diversity and inclusiveness."

Sheila nodded.

"I wanted to come to Boston, too," she said. "You know? See what it was like?"

"Whaddya think?" I said.

The power drive on Chollo's camera whirred in the background. The shutter clicked.

"It's not as liberal as I'd heard," she said.

"More repressive than we thought," Lyndon said. "But we were naïve, you know? Repression flourishes in every climate."

"Even Cambridge," Sheila said.

"So what drew you to Professor Alderson."

"There was a lot of buzz," Sheila said. "You know? I mean, he'd been in the movement since it began, almost."

"Movement?"

"The fight against imperialism, and conformity," Lyndon said. "The struggle for personal authenticity. The man was there. He was there in the sixties. He's been there."

I nodded and wrote *yikes!* in my notebook.

"The sixties," I said.

"He was at Kent State," Sheila said. "When they shot those students."

I wrote *1970?* in my notebook.

"He was with SNCC," Lyndon said. "The Weathermen, everybody."

"A hero of the counterculture," I said.

"Exactly."

"Does Professor Alderson use his experience as a basis for his seminar?"

"He'll hate it if you refer to him as *Professor Alderson,*" Sheila said. "He wants to be called Perry."

"Titles are elitist," Lyndon said. "They reinforce an oppressive system."

"Is there a Mrs. Alderson?" I said.

"If there were," Lyndon said, "he would not call her *Mrs.,* as if somehow he owned her."

"Is there anyone with whom he is sharing his life?" I said.

"Perry shares his life with many people," Sheila said. "I don't think he's ever felt any need to limit himself."

"You folks married?" I said.

"We have committed to each other," Lyndon said. "We need no stamp of acceptance from the state."

"Do you find that shocking?" Sheila said.

"No," I said. "Do you happen to have a syllabus for, ah, Perry's seminar?"

"See," Lyndon said. "You just don't get it. Perry, and by extension we, are no more bound by college structure than we are by governmental structure."

I wrote *no* in my notebook.

"Any texts?"

"The texts are being written by events," Sheila said.

"No textbooks? Grades?"

"The college has imposed pass/fail. But for Perry the only failure is the failure to be free."

"So what is class like?"

"We talk about life today as it is unfolding," Lyndon said.

"Perry helps us put it in historical perspective," Sheila said.

"Drawing upon his own experience," I said.

"Yes."

"A woman was recently killed at the college," I said. "I understand she had been dating Perry."

"Perry had been seeing her," Sheila said.

"Did you know her?"

"Casually," Lyndon said.

"Police talk to you about the killing?"

"Of course," Lyndon said. "Police. FBI. Any chance they get to bring Perry down."

"They think Perry was involved?"

"They are trying to make it look that way," Lyndon said.

"But he wasn't?"

"Of course not," Sheila said. "They just want to smear him."

"We didn't tell them one damned thing," Lyndon said. "And you can print that."

"Name, rank, and serial number."

"Exactly," Lyndon said.

"You say you knew the woman casually," I said. "You ever, ah, what, go out with them?"

"Now and then for a drink after class," Sheila said. "She was nice. She taught postfeminist literature."

I wrote *postfeminist?* in my notebook.

"I'm not comfortable," Lyndon said, "discussing this. I am not going to participate in any attempt to smear Perry."

"Of course," I said. "I don't blame you a bit. Did you know she was the wife of an FBI agent?"

"Isn't that delicious?" Sheila said. "We used to joke about it."

"Sheila," Lyndon said. He looked at her in a very unliberated way. "I don't think we should discuss this any further."

"Oh, Lyndon, don't be such a prig," she said.

Lyndon's face reddened. In my notebook I wrote *prig.*

"I'm afraid this interview is at an end," he said priggishly.

"Oh, Lyndon."

"Damn it, Sheila, be quiet. The interview is over."

I winked at Sheila.

"Free to be you and me," I said.

33.

AM BUT A poor peasant," Chollo said. "But Señor Perry seems to be a hero of the counterculture."

"Peasant?" I said.

"*Sí.*"

"You never saw a shovel in your life," I said. "You were born here. You speak better English than the president."

"Many people do," Chollo said.

"Good point," I said.

"I am simply playful," Chollo said, "like a Guadalajara armadillo."

"Armadillos are playful?"

"I do not know," Chollo said.

My cell phone rang.

Susan's voice said, "We've had an adventure."

"We?"

"Hawk and Vinnie and I," she said.

"You're okay?"

"Yes," she said.

"You're home?"

"Yes."

"I'm in Central Square," I said. "I'll be there shortly."

Which I was.

Susan had a spare room and full bath on the ground floor across the hall from her office. She occasionally used it for conferences, or now and then when she was teaching a seminar. But mostly it was empty. Hawk and Vinnie had set up in there. Susan and Pearl were in there with them. Pearl came and jumped up on me like we'd taught her not to do, and I bent low enough for her to lap my face for a while.

"*Déjà vu*," Hawk said. "Again."

"Yeah," I said. "The first go-round with the Gray Man, as I recall."

"Was," Hawk said.

Pearl tired of lapping and went back to the couch and jumped up beside Susan.

Hawk looked at Chollo.

"Chollo," Hawk said.

"Hawk," Chollo said.

Chollo looked at Vinnie and nodded. Vinnie nodded back. He had earphones on and was listening to an iPod.

Susan said, "Hello, Chollo."

She had a drink. It looked like vodka on the rocks.

"Is that vodka?" I said.

"On the rocks," she said.

I wasn't sure I had ever seen her drink vodka on the rocks. No one else was drinking.

"In honor of your adventure?" I said.

"Want to hear about it?" she said.

She was slightly drunk, which is generally as drunk as she ever gets. She wasn't slurring her speech or anything. It was more something about the eyes, some change in their look that I could never quite explain, but I knew it when I saw it.

"I do," I said.

Chollo went over and leaned on the jamb of the doorway that was open to the hall. Vinnie listened to his iPod. Hawk sat on the couch beside Susan with Pearl in between them. I pulled a chair around and straddled it backward and rested my forearms on the back.

Susan sipped some vodka.

"I went to dinner with my friend Anne Roberts," Susan said. "At the Harvest."

She sipped her drink. There were window bays on the two exterior walls of the room. Outside in late November, the afternoon had already begun to darken. There was something almost formal in the way we had composed ourselves around her in the bright room. Four rather tarnished knights and a beautiful lady in the center. Actually, the world being what it is, even the lady was maybe a little tarnished.

"Hawk and Vinnie came along behind," Susan said. "I asked them to remain discreet. Ann might have been, ah, ill at ease with a couple of bodyguards."

Pearl shifted on the couch between Hawk and Susan so that she could rest her chin on Susan's thigh. I smiled without showing it. Pearl, at least, was untarnished.

"So they stayed at the bar. After dinner we came out. Ann went to Brattle Street to walk home, and I went down the alley toward Mt. Auburn Street to get my car. There were two men at the ATM machine near the end of the alley, you know, there on the right?"

"I know," I said.

I could feel the center of my stomach begin to pinch. Susan was stroking one of Pearl's ears as she spoke.

"At the end of the alley there was a big van with a slidy side door," she said. "The door was open. When I passed the two men they suddenly grabbed me and tried to drag me into the van."

I felt the muscles in my chest and shoulders begin to clench.

"I punched one, and kneed the other one in the crotch, but it wasn't hard enough, I guess. They had me halfway into the van when Hawk and Vinnie arrived."

She looked at Hawk.

"After that it got a little confusing," she said. "I know Hawk grabbed me away from them and shoved me against the wall and pressed against me like a shield."

Hawk nodded. Susan sipped her drink, playing absently with Pearl's ear. Then she smiled.

"Actually I kind of liked that part," she said.

"They all do," Hawk said.

Vinnie remained blank, listening to his iPod.

"I get her away from them," Hawk said. "And one of them comes out with a piece and Vinnie drills him. The other one dives into the van and the van boogies with the door still open."

"Vinnie's knocking off witnesses as fast as we can discover them," I said.

Vinnie listened peacefully to his iPod. If he knew we were talking about him, he gave no sign.

"Didn't have much choice," Hawk said. "We looking after Susan."

"Yes," I said. "License plate?"

"Mass plate," Vinnie said without taking off his earphones. "ACE 310."

"Won't help," Hawk said.

I nodded.

"Probably stolen," I said.

I was looking at Susan.

"You okay?" I said.

"Yes," she said. "Me and my vodka."

"Scared?"

"Not at the time," she said. "At the time I was furious."

"Fear usually sets in later," I said.

She smiled.

"And you would know that how?" she said.

"Everybody gets scared," I said.

She looked around the room at the four of us and didn't say anything.

"I'm sorry I got you into this," I said.

"I don't like to admit this in public," Susan said. "But I'm with you. If this is part of the deal, it's worth it."

We looked at each other for a moment. I nodded.

"Chollo," I said. "You stick with Susan."

Chollo widened his eyes a little, but all he said was *"Sí."*

"And me and Vinnie?" Hawk said.

"You too," I said.

"What about you?" Susan said.

"He won't come for me as long as he doesn't know where the tapes are," I said.

"So you think this is Alderson?"

"Yes. He knows that if he gets you he can make me give him what he wants."

"So you don't think he was going to kill me?"

"No. Not until he's used you to leverage me," I said.

"But one of them pulled a gun," she said.

"Good help is hard to find," I said. "He got scared. Probably going to shoot at Hawk."

"Vinnie can't take that chance," Chollo said.

Shooter camaraderie.

"No, he couldn't," I said. "None of you can. You protect Susan. Kill anybody you have to, as soon as you need to."

I had just articulated Vinnie's guiding principle. Still listening to his iPod, he almost smiled. Then he shot at me with his forefinger.

"If you're so safe," Susan said to me, "why did you ask Chollo to come here?"

"I thought he might come in handy," I said.

"I am very handy," Chollo said. "I can shoot, I can speak Spanish, I can pick beans. And I am a very fun *hombre*."

"And we've all missed you," I said.

"*Sí*," Chollo said.

"If you give me all the protection and go it alone," Susan said, "and something happens to you, how will I feel?"

"And if I don't give you enough cover, and something bad happens, how will I feel?" I said.

"He hard to kill," Hawk said.

"What if they try to force him to give up the tapes?"

"He hard to force," Hawk said.

"I can't function unless I know you're safe," I said to Susan.

"She be safe," Hawk said.

"But why not just give him his damned tapes?" Susan said. "And wash your hands of it."

"Couple reasons," I said. "I've heard the tapes. Once he gets the tapes he'll try to kill me."

"And Doherty's wife cheated on him," Susan said.

"This needs to come out right," I said.

"*This* being what happened to Doherty recently," Susan said, "or what happened to us years ago, or both?"

"Goddamn it, Susan, this is what I do. I don't tell you how to do what you do."

Susan nodded. Had he been capable of it, Hawk might almost have looked shocked. I had probably never raised my voice to Susan in Hawk's presence. I wished I hadn't now.

"I think your work and mine may be intermingled here," she said. "But the problem is better dealt with by you than me."

147

"I'm sorry I yelled," I said.

"I know," she said. "I'm sorry I kvetched."

"I know," I said.

Chollo looked at Hawk.

"I miss something?" he said.

Hawk shook his head.

"Long time ago," Hawk said.

34.

MET EPSTEIN for breakfast at Zaftig's in Brookline.

"There's nothing closer?" I said when I sat down.

"It's close for me," Epstein said.

"You live in Brookline," I said.

"Am I Jewish?" Epstein said.

"I think so," I said.

"And I like a nice deli," he said.

"My honey is Jewish and she lives in Cambridge," I said.

"Sometimes they stray," Epstein said.

"On the other hand, she is a shrink," I said.

"But they never stray far," he said.

"Comforting, isn't it," I said. "We got anything to talk about or have you just been missing me?"

"Good to stay in touch," Epstein said. "The latkes here are fabulous."

The waitress brought us coffee, and I ordered latkes with applesauce. Epstein had eggs and onions with some sable.

"The big red-haired guy," Epstein said. "He's not in the system either."

"He didn't seem like a pro to me," I said. "He knew what he was doing, he wouldn't have dissed Chollo."

"Chollo?" Epstein said.

"Friend of mine from LA, be like dissing a cobra."

Epstein smiled.

"Remind you of me?" he said.

"No."

The waitress came with breakfast, and more coffee. I had a bite of latke.

"How are they?" Epstein said.

"How should they be?" I said.

"Fabulous," Epstein said.

"They're fabulous," I said.

Epstein nodded.

"Name's Darcy Englund," Epstein said. "AKA Red."

"I suspected that would be his nickname," I said.

"Nice to confirm it," Epstein said. "Only other thing we got is that Red's been with Alderson at least as long as Alderson's been at Concord College."

"In what capacity?" I said.

"Red?" Epstein said. "Hard to say. Friend, driver, gofer, bodyguard. We don't know. Mostly he's just around."

"Never been arrested," I said.

"Nope."

"Military service?" I said.

"Nope."

"Visible means of support."

"Last Hope," Epstein said.

"Got a job title?"

"Nope. But he deposits a two-thousand-dollar paycheck from them every week."

"Where's he live?"

"Cambridge," Epstein said. "Apartment on Hilliard Street."

"Close to Alderson," I said.

"Yep. About a block."

"You got a tail on him?"

"No," Epstein said. "He looks like small fish to me. We're sticking with Alderson."

We were quiet. I finished my latkes. Epstein finished his eggs and ate a piece of toast.

"No bagel?" I said.

"I try to avoid ethnic clichés," Epstein said.

"Like eggs and onions with a nice piece of sable," I said.

"So, sometimes I fail," Epstein said. "Whadda you got?"

"Sheila and Lyndon," I said.

Epstein nodded.

"Tell me about them," he said.

I did. Epstein took some notes on the organizations and places they had mentioned in connection with Alderson. The waitress warmed up our coffee as needed. My normal ration was two cups in the morning. I was somewhere around five this morning. Of course, they were small cups. I'd probably be able to sleep fine by the time the week was out.

"A hippie legend," Epstein said when I finished my recitation. "Perry told us he was forty-eight."

"Kent State was in 1970," I said.

"Which would have made him thirteen when it happened," Epstein said.

"Precocious," I said.

Epstein said, "We'll run it down. See how much of the legend is true. Can you give me a couple of the pictures you took?"

I nodded.

"When the truth conflicts with the legend," I said, "print the legend."

"William Randolph Hearst?" Epstein said.

"*The Man Who Shot Liberty Valance,*" I said.

"Close," Epstein said.

The waitress brought the check. Epstein picked it up.

"I got this one," he said. "You're a business expense."

"Wow, you do avoid ethnic clichés," I said.

"Jews are generous," Epstein said.

We still had coffee to drink, so we each drank some. Epstein put down his cup.

"This," he said, "has been a model of law enforcement give-and-take. Me, a representative of the Federal Bureau of Investigation. You, a simple private peep. And we share what we know to the betterment of our common interest."

"Ain't it grand," I said.

"There was another shooting in Cambridge yesterday," Epstein said. "Right in Harvard Square."

"The town too tough to die," I said.

"You wouldn't know anything about that, I suppose."

"I don't," I said.

"Some similarities to the guy got shot up in Kendall Square," Epstein said.

"The guy who killed Jordan Richmond?"

"Yeah. This guy has no identity either. We got no record of him, no fingerprints on file, no DNA. He's got no ID. The gun is unregistered."

"He had a gun," I said.

"Yeah, one I never heard of," Epstein said. "Thing was manufactured in fucking Paraguay."

"Don't see that many Paraguayan handguns," I said. "Did he have it out?"

"Yeah."

"Been fired?"

"Not recently," Epstein said.

"Where'd he get hit?" I said.

"Two in the forehead," Epstein said.

"Pretty good," I said. "Sounds like a pro."

Epstein nodded.

"Yeah," he said. "Most people aim for the middle of the mass. Gotta have confidence to shoot for the head. Especially in what looks like a gunfight. Odd how two guys with peculiar handguns and no ID get shot in the head on the street in Cambridge."

"Where'd it happen?" I said.

"Little alley next to the post office on Mt. Auburn Street."

"Not generally considered a high-risk area," I said. "What time of day?"

"Middle of the afternoon," Epstein said.

"Witnesses?" I said.

"Couple people said they saw a white van speed away right after the sound of shooting."

"That's it?" I said. "In that location? At that time of day?"

"That's it. Oddly enough, one of the postal workers got a plate number."

"And?"

"Stolen."

"Incredible," I said.

"I'm shocked," Epstein said. "Shocked, I tell you."

"And nobody saw the shooter?" I said.

Epstein looked at me for quite a long time without speaking.

Then he said, "No. Nobody saw the shooter."

35.

BECAUSE HE KNEW who I was, tailing Red was a little harder. I needed to drop off him more. And I periodically lost him because I was too far off. But I didn't mind, I just wanted to talk to him alone, in a proper location where there was privacy and space. I knew where he lived. I always found him again.

Mostly he drove Alderson places. Though never on dates. Sometimes I crossed paths with the Feds tailing Alderson. We ignored each other. The FBI guys weren't clumsy, but it is hard to stay on somebody's tail for a long time without getting noticed. I assumed Alderson knew they were there.

My time came in a couple of days. Red drove Alderson out to Taft University in Walford. The FBI and my humble self were trailing along behind them. Red dropped Alderson in front of a red-brick building on the Taft campus. There were evergreen shrubs around the building. A small neat sign out front said Hanes Science Center. A big sign on the front door said something about a conference in the auditorium about "Taking Back Your Country." There was a list of speakers. Alderson was at the top. I wondered if it was because he was important or because his name started with A.

The FBI peeled off behind Alderson, hoping to catch him saying something subversive. I stayed behind Red as he drove around a corner and parked on the top level of a four-story garage behind the Hanes building. I went in behind him and parked three cars away. We got out at about the same time. He looked at me and did a small double take.

"Whadda you doing here?" he said.

"Came to chat with you, Darcy."

He thought for a moment about my knowing his name.

Then he said, "I go by Red."

"My name was Darcy, I'd go by Red, too," I said.

"You ain't got red hair, asshole."

"You sure?" I said.

He made a brush-away gesture with one hand and started toward the elevator. I stepped in front of him.

"We need to talk, Darcy."

"You looking for trouble?" he said.

"Information," I said.

"I got no information for you," he said. "You looking for trouble, I'll be glad to accommodate you."

He tried to move past me to the elevator. I moved and blocked him again.

"How'd you happen to hook up with Alderson?" I said.

He took two handfuls of my jacket up near my neck.

"You gonna move, or am I gonna move you?" he said.

He was a big guy, bigger than I was, but jacket grabbing is an amateur move, and I suspected he'd gotten by much of his tough guy life on being big rather than skillful.

"Okay," I said. "Okay. I'll move."

He grunted and shoved me scornfully away and started past. I kicked both his ankles out from under him and he went down sideways and hard on the cement floor of the parking garage. I stepped back and waited. It took him a minute.

"You tripped me," he said. "You fucking sissy."

"Sort of," I said.

It took him a minute but he got his feet under him and got up and charged me. I moved a little and steered him past me and into the trunk of a car parked next to his. He grunted and steadied himself against the car. The impact had set off the car alarm and the horn began honking rhythmically.

"Stand still," he said. "You fight like a fucking girl."

"You think?" I said.

No one normally paid much attention to car alarms. But there might be a security guy with too much time on his hands. Best to end it. Red came after me a little more carefully now. His fists were up in front of his face. I feinted at his body with my left hand and then hooked it up over his guard when it dropped. It staggered him, and I followed with an overhand right that put him on his back. He stayed there waiting for his head to clear. When it did he sat up.

"You some kind of fucking pro?" he said.

"I am," I said.

"I don't even know what we're fighting about," he said.

"I think you wanted to show me that you could kick my ass," I said.

"And maybe I can," he said.

"Maybe," I said. "Hasn't been going too good so far."

Still sitting, Red nodded.

"Whaddya want?" he said.

"I want to talk with you."

"I ain't ratting out Perry," he said.

"No harm having some coffee," I said. "Talking about it."

He nodded. Red hadn't been knocked on his ass very often. He was trying to adjust.

"Okay," he said, and got slowly to his feet.

36.

WE WENT TO the student union and sat in the café and
had coffee. I had an apple turnover with mine. Red
chose not to eat anything. I could tell by the way he spoke that
his jaw had already started to stiffen where I popped him. It
would be quite sore at the hinge tomorrow.

"Tell me how you met Perry," I said.

"I was in a shelter," he said. "Strung out."

"What were you on?"

"Whatever I could get," he said. "And Perry would come
around to the shelter and talk to us."

"About what?"

"About how pervasive governmental repression had forced
me, all of us, into addiction and dependence," Red said. "About

how our only hope was to become independent, to be free of things that made us dependent, to stand up and say no!"

It was Red speaking, but it was Alderson's voice I was hearing.

"The government made you do it?" I said.

"Through economic manipulation."

"Like taxes?"

"Yeah, and welfare, which creates a pernicious climate of dependence that we all fall prey to."

"Pernicious," I said.

"Once you start sucking on the federal tit," Red said, "you become a federal slave. Being a drug addict is just one version of it."

"What were you doing before you became a drug addict," I said.

"I was playing football at Bowling Green. Scholarship. I failed to take advantage of the opportunity afforded me. I just played football and partied. And the partying graduated from beer to hard booze to pot to hard drugs. I dropped out and ended up on the street in Cleveland."

"How long you been straight?"

"Ten years," Red said. "No booze. No dope. It was Perry. Lotta guys thought he was just another fucking do-gooder hippie, you know? Lotta guys didn't pay him no attention. But I could hear him. I could hear what he said and I could see it right off."

"Did he work with some sort of organization in Cleveland?" I said.

"Oh, Perry, yeah, sure. He always got a organization, you know? I don't pay no attention to that. It's Perry. He's the one. He knows, man. He knows what's wrong in this country. And he is not afraid to call attention to it when he sees it. They lie to us. They don't care about us. They made up a goddamn war, to get reelected. They fucked the duck in New Orleans after the hurricane. And the country trails along behind them sucking up the handouts, doing what it's told."

I finished my turnover. It wasn't a very good turnover. But the worst turnover I'd ever eaten was excellent. And this one was far from the worst.

"So you joined up with him."

"It was like a crusade, man. It is like a crusade. Yeah, I'm with him all the way."

"You think Perry ever killed anybody?" I said.

"Of course not," Red said. "Perry's all about life."

"How about you?" I said. "You ever kill anybody?"

"No."

"If Perry asked you to, would you?"

"He wouldn't ask," Red said.

"Even if the crusade were at stake, if everything you and he and others had worked for was threatened."

"I'd do anything I had to do for Perry," Red said. "He saved my life. My spirit, man. My spirit was dead, and Perry brought it back to life."

"How about to get this audiotape he wants?" I said.

"I trust Perry, man. He says it's important to us, I believe him."

"Would you take it by force, if you had to?"

"Why not?" he said. "The culture does it to us all the time."

"The culture is sure a big pain in the ass," I said.

"You buy into it?" he said.

"Not in, not out," I said. "I like the object of my emotions to have more identity."

"Huh?"

"My girlfriend went to Harvard," I said. "Sometimes I talk funny."

"So you're saying you're on the fence," Red said. "Too many people like that. In order for evil to triumph, you know, it requires only that good men do nothing."

He said the part about evil by rote, like a kid reciting the pledge to the flag.

"Or good women," I said.

"What?"

"Don't want to sound sexist," I said.

"Oh yeah, men and women."

"Who said that thing anyway, about good men?"

"Who said it?"

"Yeah."

"Perry," Red answered.

"Did you know Jordan Richmond?" I said.

"Yeah, sure. Perry was dating her."

"Was it serious?" I said.

Red grinned and made a short chug-chug gesture with his fist.

"It was about sex?" I said.

"Perry likes the women," Red said.

"And you?" I said.

"I get my share," he said.

"Any idea who killed her?" I said.

"Jordan?"

"You know another woman been killed recently," I said.

"No."

"So any idea who killed her?"

"No."

"How about her husband?"

"Don't know nothing about him," Red said.

"If Perry needed a shooter," I said, "would he know where to get one?"

"He don't need no shooter."

"Of course not, but hypothetically, would he?"

Red looked proud.

"I know my way around," he said.

"You could get him a shooter?" I said.

"I know my way around."

I looked around the café. It was hung with Taft pennants, and pictures of Taft athletes past and present. There was a picture of Dwayne Woodcock above the big stainless coffee urns. I'd done some business with Dwayne before he went on to a big career in the NBA. I wondered what happened to him after basketball. I wondered if he could read yet, at an adult level. I wondered if he was still with Chantel. I hoped so.

"I gotta go," Red said. "Perry likes me to be around in case there's any trouble."

I nodded. He stood.

"You sucker punched me this time," he said.

"Well, for what it's worth," I said, "you take a good punch."

He looked at me for a moment.

"Yeah," he said. "Next time I'll be a little more careful."

He turned and walked out of the café. I sat around for a little while, drinking coffee and appraising the coeds, trying to be one on whom nothing is lost.

37.

WE WERE IN Susan's spare room. Vinnie was asleep on the couch.

"Red did not look like so much to me," Chollo said.

"He's big and strong," I said. "But he doesn't know how."

"Most people don't know how," Chollo said. "Guys his size don't often need to."

"'Cept they run into somebody that do," Hawk said. "You think he's a shooter?"

"Don't know," I said. "If I had to guess, I'd guess no. He sounds like a dope, except when he starts mouthing what Alderson taught him. Then he sounds like a parrot."

"How 'bout if Alderson tell him to?" Hawk said.

"He might," I said. "He thinks Alderson's divine."

"So are we," Hawk said. "And there be four of us."

Susan's office door opened and a fiftyish woman in an ankle-length black coat hurried out, not looking at anything. She went out the front door and down the steps and turned left toward Mass Ave without altering her gaze. Hanging around Susan so long, I'd learned that no eye contact was sort of *de rigueur* when departing from your shrink's office. Chollo watched her go.

"You looking at that woman's ass?" I said.

"As I mature," Chollo said, "my age limits loosen. We are very romantic, south of the border."

"Age got nothing to do with it," Hawk said. "Only two kinds of music: good and bad."

"That would be Duke Ellington," I said.

Hawk nodded.

"It would be," Hawk said.

"I'm a Desi Arnaz man, myself," Chollo said.

" 'Babalu'?" I said.

"Exactly," Chollo said. "How you going to top 'Babalu'? Duke whatssis ever do 'Babalu'?"

"God, I hope not," Hawk said.

"You putting down the music of my people?" Chollo said.

"Whenever I can," Hawk said.

As they talked neither one ever lost focus on Susan's doorway.

"You need to open your mind, my African friend. Bobby Horse, now he likes Kiowa music."

"What the hell is Kiowa music," Hawk said.

"You know. They got those pipes they play."

"You like it?"

"I never heard it. But Bobby Horse, he say it's great."

"Bobby Horse think he grew up in a damn teepee," Hawk said.

"*Sí,*" Chollo said. "And ride bareback on a pinto pony when he is still a baby. It is how he got his name."

"Only horse he ever saw he bet on," Hawk said.

"Bobby Horse is maybe a little romantic about being a Native American," Chollo said. "But he fights good."

"Yeah," Hawk said. "He do."

Susan came out of her office and walked across the hall. She was wearing a black sweater today, over a white shirt. Her pants were banker's gray and fit her very well. Her black boots had high heels. When she came into the room it seemed almost to reorganize about her. I felt what I always felt when she appeared, the *oh-boy* click in the center of my self.

"Perry Alderson just called and asked for an appointment," she said.

38.

WE ALL THOUGHT about that for a while. At least
Susan and I did. Vinnie continued to sleep. Hawk and
Chollo were impassive, waiting for Susan and me. My first reaction was *no*! My second reaction was to find Alderson and break
his back. My third reaction was the one I allowed out.

"What are you going to do?" I said to Susan.

She smiled.

"Right reaction," she said.

"What other reaction could I have?" I said.

"Oh heavens," Susan said. "I've known you too long and too
intimately . . ."

"Please," I said. "Not in front of my friends."

She smiled again.

"The other reactions would have been about you," she said.

"Not always a bad thing," I said. "Sometimes you and I are pretty inextricable."

"Yes, we are," she said. "I told him I'd see him."

"Alone?" I said.

"You know what I think about group sessions," Susan said.

"When?" I said.

"Tuesday morning, at nine-fifty."

"We got the weekend to rig the office," I said.

"Rig?" Susan said.

"Listening device, surveillance camera."

"No," she said. "I cannot spy on a patient."

"Even one who means you ill?" I said.

"We don't know that yet," she said.

From the couch, with his eyes still closed, Vinnie said, "I can put in an alarm button. I used to do electrical work."

"Under the desk," I said. "Where she can hit it with her knee?"

Susan nodded.

"That would be acceptable," she said. "And I'll have the gun you gave me. And you'll all be here."

"Why are you seeing him?" I said.

"It's what I do," Susan said. "He's there. He's of interest. I am interested."

"Doesn't this present some ethical problems for you?" I said.

"Many," she said. "I plan to explain it to him."

"About you and me?"

"Yes."

"He knows that now," I said. "Why do you think he's coming to see you?"

"That would be one of the things I'd hope to discover," she said. "I certainly won't discover anything by turning him away."

"No," I said.

"At least while he's here, we know where he is," she said.

"Will you rat him out if you learn something?" I said.

"That's not always considered good therapeutic practice," she said.

"But . . ." I said.

"I will warn him that I have some allegiance to the law," she said.

"Good," I said. "As far as he knows, I'm a sleazy gumshoe trying to blackmail him for fifty grand. That works for me."

"I won't tell," Susan said.

"Okay," I said. "Just remember he's here in order to use you to get me to give him the tapes."

"Probably," Susan said.

"But if he's going to try to leverage you," I said, "it's better that he do it here, where we can control the situation."

"If your scenario is correct," Susan said, "might he want to hold me hostage until he gets the tapes?"

"Yes."

"So killing me is not at the moment in his best interest," she said.

"No."

"And you guys will prevent him from kidnapping me."

"Yes."

"So we'll give it a try," Susan said. "See what develops."

I nodded. Susan looked around the room at the four of us, and smiled.

"Security arrangements seem impressive," she said.

Hawk said, "You ain't seen nothing yet. Wait'll Tuesday morning."

Susan looked at her watch.

"I have a client," she said.

"Who might not benefit therapeutically," I said, "from finding you hanging out with gunsels and thugs."

"This is true," Susan said and turned back to her office.

"Inextricable?" Chollo said to me when she was gone.

"*Sí,*" I said.

39.

SUSAN CAME FROM the shower into the bedroom, with a towel wrapped modestly around her. I was in bed. Pearl had settled expansively in next to me.

"Did you know I was a cheerleader at Swampscott High?" she said.

"I seem to remember that," I said.

"Sis boom bah," she said, and dropped the towel and jumped in the air, and said, "Rah, rah, rah."

"They like that at Swampscott High?" I said.

"The football team did," she said.

"The whole team?" I said.

"No, of course not," Susan said. "Varsity only. No jayvees."

Pearl was banished to the living room with a chew toy while Susan and I explored the matter of cheerleading. When she was eventually readmitted, she found a spot on the other side of Susan, and settled down to work on what was left of the chew toy.

"She used to squirm right in between us," I said.

"She's learned to respect our space," Susan said.

"Our baby's all grown up," I said.

"Yes," Susan said.

We lay quietly together in the stillness of the bedroom, listening to Pearl work on her chew toy.

"Aren't there supposed to be strings playing softly in the background," I said, "while we lie here together?"

"Pretend," Susan said.

I nodded, and closed my eyes and was quiet.

After a while I said, "It's not working. It sounds like Pearl gnawing on a bully stick."

"Won't that do?" Susan said.

"Yes," I said. "It will."

I had my arm around her shoulder. She had her head against my neck.

"Postcoital languor," she said, "is almost as good as inducing it."

"Almost," I said.

We were quiet. Pearl chewed. I could feel Susan's chest move as she breathed.

"I wonder if we should get married," Susan said.

After a moment I said, "Didn't we already try that?"

"No," she said. "We tried living together. Which was something of a disappointment."

"True," I said.

"But we didn't try marriage."

"I gather you don't see marriage as requiring cohabitation?" I said.

"No."

"It is often the case," I said.

"I know."

"So we'd continue to live as we do," I said.

"I guess," she said.

"But we'd be married," I said.

"Yes."

"And the advantage of that is . . . ?"

She rubbed her head a little against the place where my neck joined my shoulder.

"I'm not sure," she said. "I thought we might discuss it, see what we thought."

I was quiet. Pearl had finished her bully stick and was having a post-prandial nap. The room was very quiet.

"People of our generation," I said, "who feel about each other the way we feel, usually get married."

"Yes," Susan said.

"Would it make you happier?" I said.

"No . . ."

"But?"

"I guess I would feel somehow more . . . complete," she said.

"Maybe," I said. "Maybe I would, too."

We were quiet. My arm was around Susan. I rubbed her shoulder.

She said, "There are no rules, you know."

"I know."

"Regardless of how we arrange it," Susan said, "we will love each other at least until we die."

"I know."

"So if we marry or if we don't, it will not change who we are and what we feel."

"I know."

"But . . . ?"

"But there's something or other ceremonial in marriage that somehow or other matters," I said.

"I knew you'd get it," she said.

"If we decide to do it," I said, "there ought to be an interesting group at the reception."

40.

I WAS IN EPSTEIN'S OFFICE. I had brought a bag of donuts and he supplied some really awful coffee.

"You make the coffee?" I said.

"Shauna," he said. "My assistant."

"I hope she's good at other things," I said.

"Nearly everything else," Epstein said. "These donuts kosher?"

"No," I said.

Epstein nodded and took a bite.

"We looked into everywhere that Alderson was supposed to have worked his magic," he said after he'd swallowed. "Nobody ever heard of him. No record of him at Kent State. No record of any affiliation with the Weathermen, or the SDS, Peter, Paul and Mary. Nobody. Nothing."

"Maybe he's not a hero of the revolution," I said.

"If he's really forty-eight," Epstein said, "the revolution was over by the time he was old enough to be heroic."

"Maybe he lied about his age," I said.

"Why would he do that if he's claiming to be a major figure in things that were mostly over by, what, 1975?"

"We were out of Vietnam by then," I said.

"So if he's going to insist he's a hero of the era, why not claim the right age?"

"Vanity, maybe," I said.

"He wants us to think he's young?"

"Women," I said. "He likes women, and he may be so used to lying about his age to women that he does it instinctively."

"So," Epstein said. "He's either lying about his age or about his history."

"Or both," I said.

"And it appears that he has also killed two people, one of them an FBI agent," Epstein said.

"And he's working very hard to get that audiotape."

"Which isn't all that incriminating," Epstein said. "I don't think what's on that tape could even get us an arrest warrant."

"But it would cause you to investigate him," I said.

"It has," Epstein said. "And we got nothing."

"Except that he's not what he says he is," I said. "Or maybe who he says he is."

"Is that worth the risk of killing an FBI agent?" Epstein said.

"Apparently."

Epstein nodded. We were quiet for a time.

"There's something else," Epstein said.

"There's a lot else," I said.

Epstein finished a donut and drank a little coffee and made a face.

"You're right about the coffee," he said. "I'm going to have to do something about it."

"It's nice to have a manageable problem," I said.

"Yeah," Epstein said, "gives me the illusion of competence."

"So, where does a guy like Alderson get a hit man like the one who killed Jordan Richmond?" I said.

"Red?"

I shook my head.

"Red's a lummox," I said. "He's big and strong and idol-worships Alderson, or what he thinks Alderson is, but he's not a guy to arrange some murders."

"So who?"

"And why?"

We each took a second donut.

"We don't know," I said.

"Good point," Epstein said. "Why don't you work that out, and I'll deal with the coffee issue."

41.

TUESDAY WAS A clear, brisk day with just the barest possibility of snow lingering at its edges. The alarm system was installed and working under Susan's desk. Susan's office was on a corner and there were windows facing Linnaean Street, and windows on the side facing the driveway. Vinnie was in a parked car on Linnaean Street where he could see both sets of windows and the front door. Chollo was on the second floor, sitting on the top step of the front stairs. Hawk and I were in the spare room with the door open. Hawk leaned in the open doorway. I stood in the front window. I wanted Alderson to know we were around.

At quarter to ten, Perry Alderson, wearing a black pin-striped double-breasted overcoat, strolled down Linnaean Street and turned into Susan's front walk. If he saw me in the window he gave no sign. He came up Susan's steps and opened her front door and looked around her big front hall. Susan came to the office door when he entered, and said, "Come in please."

Alderson gave her a big smile and put out his hand.

"Dr. Silverman," he said. "What a pleasure. I'm Perry Alderson."

Susan shook his hand. Alderson was completely focused on her. If he saw Chollo on the stairs, or Hawk in the doorway, he reacted no more than he had to seeing me in the window, if he'd seen me in the window. They went into Susan's office and closed the door.

Hawk was motionless in the doorway where he was supposed to be. The alarm bell we had rigged was molly-anchored onto the wall next to the door. I looked at my watch. It was nine minutes to ten. Under normal circumstances Alderson would come out at twenty to eleven. I went out into the hallway. Chollo was where he was supposed to be. I looked through the cut-glass window in the front door. Vinnie was where he was supposed to be. I wasn't. I was supposed to be in the office with Susan. I walked back into the waiting room. Hawk had not moved. I looked out the front window. Vinnie hadn't moved. I could go back out in the hallway and see that Chollo hadn't moved. My options were limitless. I looked at my watch. It was now six minutes to ten.

"Susan asked me the other night if I thought we should get married," I said.

Hawk continued to look at the office door.

"How you feel 'bout that?" Hawk said.

He was dressed for business: jeans, ornate sneakers, a black sleeveless T-shirt. The big .44 Magnum revolver he favored was in a holster on his right hip. Even in repose the muscles in his arms seemed to strain against his black skin.

"I don't know."

"You love her," Hawk said. "More than I ever seen anybody love anything."

"True," I said.

Outside, the bright brisk day had gotten grayer, and the hint of snow had become a suggestion.

"So why wouldn't you?" Hawk said.

"I don't know," I said. "We wouldn't necessarily live together."

"Uh-huh."

"There won't be children," I said.

"Uh-huh."

"We have no financial reason to get married."

"Uh-huh."

"So, why would we get married?" I said.

"'Cause you love each other more than I ever seen anybody love each other," Hawk said.

"Which we've done without being married," I said.

"Or even living together," Hawk said.

"We tried that," I said.

"I remember," Hawk said. "Probably a good idea not to do that again."

"Yes."

I looked at my watch. It was three minutes after ten.

"So what you going to do?" Hawk said.

"We'll talk about it some more. I guess if she wants it bad enough we'll do it."

"You know why she want it?" Hawk said.

"Not exactly," I said.

"You going to ask her?"

"I thought maybe I should get it clear in my own head first."

"How that going?" Hawk said.

I shrugged.

"You ever think about getting married?" I said.

"No," Hawk said.

"Would you ever?" I said.

"I don't believe in much," Hawk said.

"And I do?" I said.

"You a bear for symbols and shit," Hawk said. "You think about what stuff means."

"And getting married means something."

"It do," Hawk said.

I walked past him out into the hall again and looked up the stairs at Chollo, and then out the front-door window at Vinnie. I turned and looked at Hawk and nodded my head slowly.

"Yeah," I said. "It do."

Then I went back in the spare room and stood near the door and waited.

42.

AFTER APPROXIMATELY EIGHTEEN MONTHS, 11:40 rolled around and Susan's office door opened. Alderson stepped into the hall and turned and shook Susan's hand, as he had when he'd come in.

"Susan," he said. "Thank you so much. This has been one of the most remarkable hours I've ever spent."

Susan shook his hand and nodded.

"Next Tuesday," she said.

"Same time, same place," Alderson said.

He turned for a moment and looked at me and smiled and turned back and went out the front door. Susan continued to stand in her office doorway. I went to the front window and watched him go down the steps and along the front walk and turn right and head back up Linnaean Street the way he had come.

We gathered in the spare room. Hawk and I on straight chairs. Vinnie on the couch with his iPod. Vinnie didn't care if Alderson was unusual. If he needed to be shot, Vinnie would shoot him. Otherwise Vinnie liked listening to his iPod. Chollo sat beside Vinnie on the couch. It was hard to tell what interested Chollo, but he always seemed to pay attention. Susan rested her good-looking butt on the edge of the conference table.

"He's a very unusual man," Susan said.

"You have a moment to share your thoughts?" I said.

"I have all day," Susan said. "I didn't know how it would go, so I cleared my calendar after his visit."

"Didn't want no patients around, case we had to kill him," Hawk said.

"Yes," Susan said.

Chollo smiled and nodded at her.

"Thoughtful," he said. "For a gringette."

"Is that a female gringo?" Susan said.

"It is what we always said in my village."

"Village?" I said. "What village is that?"

"Bel Air," Chollo said. "Bobby Horse and me, we live in Bel Air with Mr. Del Rio."

"A hardscrabble life," I said.

"*Sí.*"

We were quiet, everybody but Vinnie looking at Susan, waiting for her to tell us what she could. We knew she had all sorts of arcane shrink considerations hemming her in, so we didn't know quite what to ask her.

"Did you give him your disclaimer?" I said. "About me?"

"Yes."

"How did that sit with him?"

"He simply nodded," Susan said.

"No comment?"

"None. Beyond the nod, it was as if I had not mentioned it," she said. "He never referred to you in our conversation."

"He gave me one smile, when he was leaving," I said.

"Why do you suppose he did that?" Susan said.

"To show that he saw me there, and I didn't matter," I said. She nodded.

"What do you think?" I said.

"First," she said, "I am quite sure he's fraudulent."

"There's nothing wrong with him?" Hawk said.

"Oh, there's a great deal wrong with him, I'm sure," Susan said. "But he's not here seeking help with it."

"Shocking," Chollo said.

"Can you tell why he's here?"

"I would guess that he's here to seduce me," Susan said.

"Him too?" I said.

She smiled.

"I think," she said, "that the seduction, in this instance, is the means, not the purpose."

"The purpose being?"

"To get control of you," she said.

I nodded.

"Is there any chance that his visit to you was legit?" I said.
She shrugged.

"My business is pretty much like yours." She glanced at the men in the room and smiled. "Minus the firepower. There are a lot of informed guesses made."

"And your informed guess is that he's not seeking therapy," I said.

"Correct."

"So you may feel less constrained than you might otherwise feel to protect the privacy of the session."

She smiled again.

"Correct," she said. "To a point."

"How will you know when you reach the point," I said.

"I'll know," Susan said.

"So what he talk 'bout," Hawk said.

"He was effusive," Susan said, "when he came in. He'd heard so many wonderful things about me. He hadn't expected anyone so attractive. He hoped he wouldn't bore me."

Through the front window I could see an inconsequential flurry of snow drift past.

"I told him," Susan said, "that people easily bored by others didn't usually enter this profession, and perhaps he might tell me why he had come. He began by telling me about his father. There's nothing unusual in that. Many people come and begin by telling me about their parents and assume I will see the problem and tell them what to do. It's not very effective, but it's common, and it's often useful as kind of a warm-up, before the game starts."

"Did you believe what he told you?"

"I don't know if it was true or not," she said. "He appeared to admire his father. And he feared he couldn't live up to him."

"Not an unheard-of problem," I said.

"No, in fact," Susan said, "it is so common that one is a little suspicious of it when it surfaces fully expressed, so to speak, ten minutes into your first therapy session."

"You think he made it up?"

"I have no idea. But he has certainly articulated it before."

"You think he's seen a shrink before?" I said.

"I would guess that he has," Susan said. "He seems comfortable with it. He seemed to know how it worked. He's not nervous. No uncomfortable jokes about the couch or all shrinks taking August off. He was very at ease, very articulate. And he had an agenda. He wasn't uncertain. He knew where he wanted to go in the interview."

"How did he present his seductive side?" I said.

Hawk looked at Chollo.

"You see how he ease in on that?" Hawk said.

"More subtle than the plumed serpent," Chollo said.

"The plumed serpent live in Bel Air, too?" I said.

"*Sí.*"

"It was mostly attitude and body language," Susan said. "Most women recognize it. The appraising look. The eye contact. The implication of specially shared knowledge. Taking any opportunity to flatter my appearance. You often say you can tell if a woman is, ah, compliant."

"I can."

"Same thing," Susan said.

"All men are compliant," I said, "in your case. If they're straight."

"In fact," Susan said, "that's not always so. But it was so here."

"Did he make a specific proposal."

"No. But he made an appointment for next Tuesday and he acted as if he were in for the long haul."

"The therapy or the seduction?" I said.

"Both," she said. "One being the means to the other."

"Levels within levels," I said.

"Pretend therapy," Susan said, "in order to pretend seduction, so that he can get control of you, so that he can prevent you from whatever exactly it is he wants to prevent you from doing."

Chollo smiled.

"I am not sure, *señorita*, that the seduction part is pretend," he said. "It would be deceitful, but I believe he would be very happy to carry it off while he was at it."

"Why, Chollo," Susan said. "How gallant."

"I too am compliant," Chollo said.

Susan smiled a wide smile.

"I knew that," she said.

43.

SUSAN HAD DINNER with three women friends at the Bristol Lounge in the Four Seasons Hotel. Vinnie and Chollo had the evening off. Hawk and I sat at the bar and nursed one beer each, and watched out for Susan.

"What the two gunslingers doing?" Hawk said.

"Vinnie is showing Chollo the town," I said.

"How you like to be seeing the town with Vinnie?" Hawk said.

"Not fun like with you and me," I said.

Hawk looked at his half-drunk glass of beer getting warm and flat in front of him.

"What could be more fun than you and me?" Hawk said.

"Swapping jokes with Don Trump?" I said.

"Well, yeah," Hawk said. "That would be more fun."

Susan stood and said something to her friends. I slid off the bar stool. She turned and strolled toward the ladies' room. Several people, men and women, turned and looked at her. In her understated shrink uniform she was stunning. Out with friends, she was flamboyantly so. I caught up with her at the ladies' room door.

"Here's what I want you to do," I said. "You go in and look around and come back and report to me. Is there a window? Is there another way in or out? Who else is in there? If you are not back out here in one minute from the time you go in, I'm coming in after you."

"One minute?"

"Plenty of time to do what I ask."

"Isn't this a little overproduced?" she said.

"Better too much than too little," I said.

She nodded.

"Okay," she said, "here I go."

As she went in, I looked at my watch. It took her twenty-eight seconds to reconnoiter and report.

"No one else is in here. There are two full toilet stalls. Floor to ceiling. Both doors are ajar. There is neither a window nor another way in or out."

I nodded.

"Can you get everything done in there in five minutes?" I said. "Including standing in front of the mirror and poking at your hair?"

"If I must," she said.

"After five minutes," I said, "I come in."

"If there are too many more rules and ultimatums I may not be able to go," she said.

I smiled and bowed her back into the ladies' room. Two women came by a minute and sixteen seconds later. They looked at me in mild askance as I leaned against the wall beside the door. I shrugged and smiled. They went past me in silence and entered the ladies' room. Two minutes later Susan came out.

"I didn't even look in the mirror," she said. "Just washed my hands and came right out."

"I don't believe you," I said.

She smiled.

"I didn't look very long," she said.

She walked back to her table and sat down. I walked on to the bar.

"Fella wanted your seat," Hawk said. "I told him it was taken."

"He give you a hard time?" I said.

Hawk smiled. I nodded.

"Probably thought he was brave to ask," I said.

"Was," Hawk said.

We sat looking at the handsome room, full of handsome people, most of whom were handsomely dressed. No one appeared dangerous, which didn't mean that nobody was. Especially us.

"Susan mentioned that Perry Alderson seemed to have some experience with psychotherapy," I said.

"She did," Hawk said.

"Red told me that he met Perry when he was down and out in Cleveland and Perry did some street counseling," I said.

"He say who Perry worked for?" Hawk said.

"No."

"FBI got any info on him in Cleveland?" Hawk said.

"No. "

"Don't mean there is no info," Hawk said.

"It don't," I said.

"Do mean somebody got to go get it?" Hawk said.

"It do," I said.

We both watched Susan in animated conversation with three other women. They were all attractive women, but they all seemed pallid in Susan's penumbra.

"Here's how I figure," Hawk said.

"Uh-huh?"

"You a detective and I'm not. I don't detect as well as you. Could be a detective, a course, if I wanted. But I don't. On the other hand I can bust somebody's ass, 'bout as well as you, maybe better."

"So I should go to Cleveland," I said.

"Yes."

"I'm not buying the equality-of-ass-busting argument," I said. "But you are certainly in the top two."

"We know that one of us be the best," Hawk said. "Just don't agree on who."

"You have to be with her every day, all day, every night, all night. You can never be any further away from her than you are right now. Vinnie and Chollo do wonderful work. But they are backup. You're the one."

"I know," Hawk said.

We both looked at her. She finished a story with her arms out and raised toward the ceiling. The table burst into laughter. Hawk smiled.

"I'll stay as close as you do," he said.

"Almost as close," I said.

"*Almost* make all the difference," Hawk said. "Don't it?"

"It does," I said. "But I suppose if I were truly enlightened I'd say that would all be pretty much up to her."

"But you not that enlightened," Hawk said.

"No," I said.

"Me either," Hawk said.

We were quiet again, watching the table of women. Women seemed so much more at ease in social groups than men did. Men were okay in project groups, where they had a common goal and vocabulary. Sports teams. Combat units. Construction crews. Guarding Susan. But six guys all dressed up having dinner together was usually a sorrowful sight.

"I know we talked 'bout it before," Hawk said. "And I know you not going to go for it. But . . . any one of us, Vinnie, Chollo, me, be happy to clip Alderson for you. Chollo could do it and be back in Bel Air for cocktails before the cops found the body."

"I gotta do it," I said.

"Clip him?"

"No, I gotta even this up."

"Nothing says *even* like two in the head," Hawk said.

"Not my style."

"'Less you has to," Hawk said.

I nodded.

"I've had to," I said. "So far, not this time."

"This ain't just about Doherty," Hawk said.

"Whatever it's about," I said, "I'm going to clear it."

"It about Susan and the guy she took off with two hundred years ago," Hawk said.

"Whatever it's about," I said, "I'm going to clear it."

44.

I T TOOK TWO HOURS to fly to Cleveland, and thirteen hours to
drive there. I drove. Route 90 all the way. There is nothing to
equal a long boring drive alone for clearing the head. And mine
needed clearing. Out the Mass Pike. Through the Berkshires.
Onto the New York Thruway. Through Buffalo. Down along the
eastern shore of Lake Erie. Through Erie. To Cleveland.

It was dark when I got there, and my head was so clear as to
be empty. I checked in, unpacked, went to the bar and had a
sandwich and a couple of beers, went back up to my room, and,
exhausted from the excitement, went to bed.

In the morning I went out and looked for Red's shelter. I had
a list of shelter addresses I'd gotten by phone Monday, from the
Department of Public Health. Epstein had supplied head shots

of Red and of Alderson, blown up and enhanced, from surveillance photos. I was wearing a Red Sox hat to be provocative, and a leather jacket to be warm. I was alert. I had a gun. I was everything a slick Boston private eye should be when patrolling the street shelters in Cleveland.

I liked Cleveland. It was no longer the mistake on the lake, when the river caught fire, and so did the mayor. There was a new ballpark, and a new arena. The downtown was alive. The flats were more so. There had always been a kind of magisterial, real city architectural dignity about Cleveland. It was still dignified, but now it was also lively.

Where I was looking, however, the liveliness, if any, was chemically induced. Mostly there was torpor. Except for the people who staffed the shelters. They seemed sincere and sufficient. Though most of them seemed sort of tired, too.

My third day in Cleveland was bright and hard cold, with a wind off the lake. In mid-afternoon, some distance out Euclid Avenue, in the basement of a dingy church that might once have been a furniture store, I found a shelter where a staffer recognized Red when I showed his picture. Her name was Cora. Black. Kind. Tired. Pretty tough.

"I don't know his real name," she said. "We called him Red. He was a kid, really, big as he was. There was something forlorn about him. Did he make it?"

"He's sober," I said. "Gainfully employed."

"How come you're asking about him?"

"I'm investigating someone who might have counseled him," I said, and showed her Alderson's picture.

196

"Oh, sure," she said. "Dr. Alderson."

"Tell me about him," I said.

We were in a large empty basement filled with cots. On each cot was a pillow and a folded blanket. In the far corner of the room was a small kitchen setup: stove, refrigerator, sink, cupboards. Something in an industrial-sized pot was simmering on the stove. A man in a white T-shirt was sweeping up. Tattoos covered his skinny arms.

"Dr. Alderson was a professor at Coyle State. Psychology. He used to come by couple evenings a week. Talk with some of the shelter folks. He spent a lot of time, I remember, with Red."

"You pay him?" I said.

"No, no. We got no money for paying," Cora said. "Everybody volunteers here, 'cept me. I'm full-time staff."

"How big a staff is it?" I said.

She smiled.

"Me," she said.

"Place looks pretty good," I said.

"We got rules. Blankets have to be folded. Floors have to be swept. Plates and stuff have to be washed, and if you don't take your turn, you're out."

"Ever have any trouble here?"

"No," she said. "Couple of cops come in every night, have coffee, look around. I don't tolerate no trouble."

"What else can you tell me about Dr. Alderson?" I said.

"It's been a while," Cora said. "Don't remember much to speak of. Just that he was good. He come regular. Would sit and talk with some of these people. Listen to what they had to say."

"He save many besides Red?" I said.

"Not much that's savable," Cora said. "Time they here most of them pretty far down the chute. Even if you could get them straight, they got substance-abuse problems, dementia, liver problems, cancer. They not going anywhere."

"Did he spend as much time with those kinds of people?"

"I don't know. Evenings are pretty busy here. Helped Red, though. I can remember that."

"Can you give me an address for Coyle State?" I said.

"Cabbie'll know," she said.

"I'm driving."

"Rental car?"

"Nope, my own. I drove out here."

"From Boston?" she said.

"Yep."

"You 'fraid to fly?"

"Nope."

"Why you drive here from Boston?"

"Gave me time to think," I said.

"I'll bet it did," she said.

She wrote out an address on the top sheet of a small yellow pad, tore off the sheet, and gave it to me.

"You getting rich here?" I said.

She smiled again.

"Not hardly," she said.

"So why do you do it?"

"Might as well be me," she said.

"Nobody better," I said, and put out my hand.

45.

LAY ON MY BED in the Holiday Inn and talked with Susan on the phone.

"Hawk on the job?" I said.

"If he stayed any closer we'd be having sex," Susan said.

"Yikes," I said.

"Sort of a metaphor," Susan said. "He's very conscientious."

"Vinnie and Chollo?"

"Right behind Hawk," Susan said. "In truth they're driving me crazy."

"Good," I said.

"I know. I'm very safe."

We were quiet. It didn't feel like quiet. It felt like we were saying things to each other.

After a moment, Susan said, "Progress today?"

"Yeah, some," I said. "I found someone who knew Alderson. He was associated with a college out here. I'm going there tomorrow."

"What college?"

"Coyle State," I said.

"Nope," Susan said. "Never heard of it."

"Now you have," I said. "You can always learn things talking to me."

"Yes," Susan said. "It's one of the reasons I do it."

I looked up at the ceiling. It was a standard sprayed-on ceiling. The room was generic hotel chain, generic furniture, generic rug. Nice view of the lake if I stood up. I'd been in a lot of rooms like this, mostly minus the view. They worked fine. They housed you, kept you warm, let you bathe and sleep and eat. They didn't do much for the soul, but their mission had nothing to do with the soul.

"Any other reasons?" I said.

"Yes," she said. "Do you know when you're coming home?"

"No. It'll depend a little on what I find out at the college tomorrow."

"Have you been thinking about us?" she said.

"Yes," I said.

"Have you been thinking about marriage?"

"Yes."

"And?"

"We are the kind of people who marry," I said.

"Yes."

"On the other hand there's nothing broken."

"So why fix it?" Susan said.

"Maybe," I said.

Again the interactive quiet stretching nearly seven hundred miles across the dark fields of the republic. The fields were now probably darker and fewer than the ones Fitzgerald imagined, but I liked the phrase.

"And have you been thinking about why you're so committed to this case?" Susan said.

"Most of the drive out here," I said. "When I wasn't thinking about marriage."

"Any conclusions?"

"More a bunch of images," I said. "Doherty talking about his wife. The look on his face when he listened to the tape. The way his wife seemed to feel he didn't matter."

"And are there any images of us that pop up?"

"We were separated," I said. "I had to kill some people in a way I don't feel so good about."

"And if I hadn't done what I did, you wouldn't have had to kill the people you killed."

"True."

"Isn't that a little hard to forgive?" Susan said.

"I've never thought so," I said.

"Until this case?" Susan said.

"Doherty has to matter to someone," I said.

"He matters to Epstein," Susan said.

I didn't say anything.

"I did a number of things that caused us both a lot of pain."

"It did," I said. "But we got past that."

"I have never liked talking about it," Susan said. "But I did what I had to do at the time."

"Me too," I said.

"Would it help if we talked about it now?"

"I don't think so," I said.

Again the rich silence across the phone connection.

"I love you," she said. "You know that. I have always loved you. Even when I couldn't stand to be with you, and was with someone else, I loved you."

"It didn't always feel quite that way," I said.

"No, I'm sure it didn't," she said. "But it was true. You have to know it was true. That it is true."

"I know," I said.

"Don't forget it," she said.

After we hung up I stood in the window and looked at the dark lake stretching north to the horizon and beyond it to Canada. There was a moon, and I could see some sort of isolated bell buoy marking something a half mile from shore.

"I won't forget it," I said.

46.

COYLE STATE COLLEGE was a scatter of yellow brick buildings across from a shopping center in Parma. The vice president for administration was a guy with a bad comb-over.

"Gerald Lamont," he said when we shook hands. "Call me Jerry."

Jerry was wearing a plaid sport coat, with a maroon shirt and tie. It went perfect with the comb-over.

"I'm interested in a member of your faculty from ten years ago, Perry Alderson."

"Sure," he said.

He picked up the phone and dialed an extension.

"Sally? Could you look up a former faculty member here, from ten years ago, Perry . . ."

He looked at me and raised his eyebrows.

"Alderson," I said.

"Perry Alderson, yeah, soon as you can. Thanks, Sal."

He hung up.

"What'd this guy Perry do?"

"Just a name that came up in a case back in Boston," I said.

"Red Sox Nation," Jerry said.

"That's right," I said.

"It was great for you guys in 2004," Jerry said. "I think the whole country was rooting for you."

"It was great," I said.

Jerry's phone rang.

"Hi, Sal. You're sure? How about a few years either side? No? Okay."

He hung up and looked at me and shook his head.

"No Perry Alderson," he said.

"Teaching assistant?"

"We have never had a sufficient graduate program for teaching assistants."

"The college have a program," I said, "for counseling street people at the Church of the Redeemer, on Euclid?"

"I don't think so," Jerry said.

I didn't have the sense that Jerry was on top of things here at Coyle.

"Did they ten years ago?" I said.

"Ten years ago I was working for the Ohio Department of Education," Jerry said. "Lemme call my assistant dean. She was here then, I think."

He picked up the phone and dialed.

"Hi. Lois? Could you come down to my office? Yes. Please. Now. Okay, thanks."

"You don't have this kind of information on computers?" I said.

"I'm not a computer guy," he said.

Assistant Dean Lois came into the office. She was a great improvement on Jerry. Jerry introduced us, and explained me.

"I'm interested in a guy named Perry Alderson. Said he was a professor here about ten years ago. Psychology."

Lois shook her head.

"I've been here for twenty years," she said. "First four as a student. I was a psych major. After graduation I stayed on as an administrator. I don't remember a Perry Alderson."

If she was a freshman twenty years ago she'd be in her late thirties now. A fine age for a woman. I took my picture of Perry Alderson out and put it on the desk.

"Either of you recognize him?" I said.

They both looked. Jerry shook his head.

Lois said, "My God, that's Bradley Turner."

"Bradley Turner," I said.

"Yes," Lois said. "I used to date him. Though I guess I wasn't alone in that."

"Active ladies' man?" I said.

"Very," she said.

"Tell me about him," I said.

"This place used to be a junior college," Lois said. "Two years to an associate's degree. Then when we joined the state college system, we moved to a full four-year curriculum and added a small graduate program offering a master's degree in social work and psychology."

"The master's was terminal?" I said.

"Yes. We did not, still don't, offer a Ph.D. We don't have the resources."

"We're headed in the right direction," Jerry said.

Both Lois and I nodded. I had already figured out what Lois had long known about Jerry.

"Was Bradley in the graduate program?"

"Yes. He was older. Said he had been deeply engaged in the peace movement for many years, but now had decided that there was a better way. He was working toward a master's in pysch and deprivation counseling."

"Deprivation counseling," I said.

"It's a program to which we lay original claim," Jerry said. "Working with the impoverished, those challenged by drugs and alcohol. They have special problems, and we feel that there needs to be specialized training."

"Turner was in that program," I said to Lois.

"Yes. I was too. That's how I met him. We had classes together."

"While you two are talking," Jerry said, "I'll go and see if Sally can dig up this guy Turner's record."

"Good," I said.

Jerry got up and went out.

"And now you're working with the impoverished here at Coyle State?" I said.

She smiled.

"The reality of impoverishment is much nastier than the academic hypothesis," Lois said. "I decided college administration was more my line."

"Speaking of nasty," I said.

"Very nasty," she said. "But here, at least, no one has the fortitude to be really dangerous."

I nodded.

"How old would you say he was at the time?" I said.

"Late thirties. It was part of what made him fascinating. Remember, I was like nineteen. He would talk about his adventures in the peace movement the way some men tell war stories. Haight-Ashbury. Kent State. SNCC. All that. Names. Songs. He was like a legendary figure."

"So he'd be in his late fifties now," I said.

"Yes. Isn't that amazing?"

"Why'd you break up?" I said.

"My tendencies are monogamous," she said. "I got tired of sharing him."

"Did you have to share him with many?" I said.

"Every."

I nodded.

"When's the last time you saw him?" I said.

"Oh, God, I don't know," she said. "He stuck around one more year after I graduated, working on his master's. It was slow. He only took a few courses, like one a semester."

"Did he ever tell you where he was from?"

"California. I think Los Angeles, or around there."

"What had he been doing between the end of the revolution and the time you knew him?" I said.

"He would have answered that the revolution was ongoing. That the impoverished were the victims of an oppressive government."

"No doubt," I said. "But what was he doing?"

"He implied that he was slowly putting together the elements for a new movement," she said. "But I don't really know that. He was always mysterious about his past, which I loved. It made him quite exotic."

Jerry came back into the room looking perplexed. My guess was that Jerry was often perplexed. This time, however, he appeared to have good reason.

"There's no record," he said, "of Bradley Turner ever being enrolled here."

"Hot damn," I said.

47.

JERRY HAD A MEETING he had to attend. So we went to
Lois's office, which was smaller. We didn't mind. We had
probably used up pretty much all that Jerry had already.

"He must have just come to classes," Lois said. "Just walked
in and sat down and acted like he was a student."

"Thirst for knowledge?" I said.

She shrugged.

"Good place to meet girls?" she said.

"Sort of a reversal of the norm," I said.

Lois smiled.

"Yes," she said. "Most students are enrolled and act like
they're not."

"Do you know any other people who would remember Turner/Alderson?" I said.

She smiled slightly.

"Women," she said. "It would be nearly all women."

"Names?" I said.

"Oh, God," she said. "We're talking about fifteen, twenty years ago."

I nodded. She looked at me speculatively. Then she picked up the phone and dialed.

"Ruth? Lois . . . I'm fine . . . absolutely . . . can you send me a list of the members of my class, when I was here? . . . yes, and maybe the class on either side of me? . . . yes . . . real soon . . . thank you."

She smiled at me.

"Alumni secretary. She'll send the names over, maybe jog my memory."

"And maybe some current addresses," I said.

"I'm sure," Lois said.

She was still looking at me, like an appraiser.

"You're not a regular police detective," she said.

"Private," I said.

"So people hire you," she said.

"If they're wise," I said.

"Who hired you to find Brad Turner?"

"It's sort of the outgrowth," I said, "of something else I'm working on."

"And you're not going to tell me what that something else is," she said.

"Try not to," I said.

She got a pad of blue-lined white paper out of her drawer.

"You don't have to," she said.

"Thanks."

She kept looking at me.

"I suppose it's not like on TV," she said.

"Actually, it's just like that," I said.

She laughed.

"Sure it is," she said.

She doodled a little smiley face on the pad.

"I have to say, though, you look like a private detective," she said.

"What do they look like?" I said.

"Big, strong, intrepid, handsome, in a rough way."

"Yeah," I said. "That's accurate."

"And," she said, "you're fun."

I nodded.

"Bubbly," I said.

A pale young woman with red-framed eyeglasses came in and handed Lois a thick printout of names and addresses.

"Ms. Carter sent these over," the young woman said, and hurried out as if she were escaping.

Lois looked at the paper.

"Well," she said. "Let's see."

48.

I HAD BOUGHT myself a bottle of Dewar's scotch and was having some with soda and ice, sitting on the bed in my hotel room, looking at the gray lake, talking to Susan.

"So something happened," I said, "between the time Lois the assistant dean knew him as Bradley Turner, and the time Red met him as Perry Alderson."

"Which is what kind of time frame?" Susan said.

"She knew him twenty years ago. Red tells me that Perry straightened him out and he's been straight for ten years."

"That's a pretty big gap to fill," Susan said. "Ten years."

"I'll narrow it, I suspect, when I've plowed through Lois's list of names."

"How many?" Susan said.

"Sixteen," I said. "All women."

"Hmmm."

"Chance to polish up my seductive charm," I said.

"It's shiny enough," Susan said.

"You should know," I said.

"I do."

"I promise to use it," I said, "only for professional purposes."

"Oh good," she said.

"Who's with you?" I said.

"Everybody."

"Hawk?"

"Yes. He and Chollo and Vinnie are going to have dinner with me."

"Where?"

"Here," she said.

"You cooking?"

"Almost," she said.

"Almost?"

"Well, I'm setting the table, and making everything look lovely."

"So who's cooking?"

"Chollo," she said.

"Chollo?"

"Yes. He says he's going to make us an authentic south-of-the-border meal."

"Out of what?" I said.

"I don't know. He went shopping this afternoon while Hawk and Vinnie were, ah, on duty."

"Shopping," I said.

"*Sí*," she said.

"Jesus," I said. "He's got you doing it."

I could hear the amusement in her voice.

"He says that in his village the roots of the corn culture go deep."

"He lives in Bel Air," I said. "He thinks the corn culture is Wild Turkey on the rocks."

"Right now he's peeling avocados," Susan said.

"Well," I said. "There are things Chollo does that no one I've ever seen can do better."

"Even Vinnie?"

"Even him," I said.

"Have you seen him cook?"

"No."

"I'll report tomorrow on the results," she said. "Are you going to share with Epstein the facts of Alderson's other name?"

"Not right now," I said.

"How did I know that?" Susan said.

"Because you went to Harvard?"

"Maybe," she said. "Or maybe because I have an advanced degree in you."

"Are you embarrassed to tell me you love me?" I said. "In front of your dinner companions?"

"I love you," she said. "It is the strongest feeling I have ever had."

"You're sure they can't hear me?" I said.

"Sure," she said.

"I love you, too," I said.

49.

CLAIRE GOLDIN was the sixth name that Lois had given me. Like the previous five, and probably the next ten, she had dated the former Bradley Turner during her college years. And in her case, for several years after. We met for coffee in Tower City. She had a noticeable body and blond highlights in her hair.

"I didn't care that he was endlessly promiscuous," she said and smiled at me. "So was I."

"Was?" I said.

"Sorry," she said.

"Always a day late," I said. "And a dollar short."

"But I had a rule against married men, and I found out he was married."

"Who was he married to?"

"I don't know. But he always came to my place, we never went to his. And I sort of wondered about that. Then I saw a man following us. I saw him a couple of times. There was no reason for anybody to follow me." She grinned again. "For crissake, I hadn't even been married yet."

"You're married now," I said.

"Third time. I'm trying to make it work."

"Love?" I said.

"Enhanced by money," she said. "Anyway, I asked Brad about it, the guy following us. And he said it was the government. That they'd been trying to get something on him ever since he was first active in the movement."

"Did he mention anything specific?"

"No. And I didn't ask. I'm just a simple sexpot," she said.

"I like that in a woman," I said.

She laughed.

"I'll bet you do," she said. "And you look like you could handle it."

"Years of training," I said.

She laughed again.

"So I didn't know anything about the movement, and still don't," she said. "But I got the license plate number on the car, and I have a brother who's a cop in Toledo. So I asked him to find out who the guy was."

"And?"

"My brother says it's not the government at all. It's a guy named Fred Schuler, who lists his occupation as private investigator. So my brother called him and Schuler tells him that he's been hired by Brad's wife to see if he's faithful."

"Just like that?" I said.

"I think my brother threatened him a little." She smiled. "Big brother, you know?"

"Did you ask Turner about this?" I said.

"Hell no," she said. "I got places to go, people to see. There were plenty more where he came from."

"Did you say good-bye?"

She shook her head.

"I stopped returning his calls," she said. "After a couple of tries, he stopped calling."

"So you never talked to him again after your brother told you about the private eye."

"Correct," she said.

"And that would have been when?" I said.

She leaned her head back a little and closed her eyes to think.

"I graduated in 1990," she said, her head still tilted, her eyes still closed. "And we stayed in touch . . ."

She opened her eyes and nodded. She had very big eyes and she made them up well. I had long observed that big eyes were a definite fashion plus.

"About four years after graduation," she said, "1994, early summer. I remember we were sitting outside at a café when I first spotted the guy following us."

I had a small notebook and I wrote down *Claire Goldin* and the year, *1994*.

"And you still remember Fred Schuler's name," I said.

"It reminded me of that football coach," she said.

"Don Shula?"

"Yes. Did you know he once played for the Browns?" she said.

"Don Shula," I said.

"Yes."

"Not Fred Schuler?"

"You're silly," she said.

"Admittedly," I said. "Did you ever go see Fred Schuler?"

"No."

"And you haven't seen nor heard from Bradley Turner since?"

"No."

I took out a business card and handed it to her.

"If you have any other thoughts," I said.

"Sure," she said.

"And good luck with the current marriage," I said.

She took the card and read it and smiled.

"Plus," she said, "if it doesn't work out, I have your card."

"Bench strength is good," I said.

50.

LAY ON THE BED in my hotel room with the phone to my ear.

"Chollo did make the guacamole," Susan said, "but the rest of his shopping turns out to have been takeout from José's, which he reheated."

"He cooks like you do," I said.

"Except for the guacamole," Susan said.

"Hard to imagine you peeling an avocado," I said.

"Peeling avocados is icky," Susan said. "And there's a big, hideous stone in the middle."

"I know," I said. "Did you have another appointment with Alderson?"

"Yes."

"Everybody where they should have been?"

"Vinnie outside. Chollo upstairs. Hawk in the study. My alarm system in place. My gun in the desk drawer."

"Loaded."

"Of course."

"The drawer open wide enough to reach the gun," I said.

"Of course," Susan said. "Remember, I have a Harvard Ph.D."

"Comforting," I said. "What's he doing in there?"

"He's charming me," Susan said.

"Has it occurred to him that others may have tried that?"

"No," Susan said. "I don't think it has."

"As far as I can tell," I said, "he's had great success with it in the past."

"I would imagine he has," Susan said.

"Is he talking about matters of substance with you?" I said.

"It's all substance," Susan said. "No matter what they say. Even if he's lying, it is of substantial interest to see why he chose those lies."

"Is he still talking about his father?" I said.

"Yes, and his father's heroism in the protest movement, and of his own attempts to emulate it."

"But?"

"But if he's forty-eight he'd be awfully young for it, and his father would almost certainly be older than the average sixties protester."

"In fact he appears to be about fifty-five," I said.

"The math works even worse," Susan said.

"Isn't that dumb?" I said. "To make up a story that doesn't make sense in terms of simple chronology?"

"It may be. But troubled people often fuse themselves with a parent or someone else when they are talking about themselves."

"So is he troubled?"

"Yes. But he's not talking about what's troubling him," Susan said.

"You have a thought what that might be?" I said.

She laughed.

"You, probably," she said.

"I'm not sure you can help him with that," I said.

"Nor wish to," Susan said. "But none of that is germane to what he's doing. Right now he just wants to seduce me into being alone with him."

"Which will not happen," I said.

"Which will not happen," Susan said. "What progress are you making?"

"I have talked to sixteen women that Alderson knew when he was in Cleveland. The most recent one to see him was Claire Goldin, who last saw him in 1994 when his name was still Turner."

"When did Red meet him?" Susan said.

"Somewhere around 1996," I said. "When his name had changed to Alderson."

"So whatever caused him to change his name happened between 1994 and 1996," Susan said. "Are you ready to talk with Epstein yet?"

"No."

"The FBI has considerable resources. They might be able to find out a little about Bradley Turner."

"Do I tell you how to shrink the loonies?" I said.

"Wow," Susan said. "I've never heard it described that way."

"One of the women I talked to told me I was fun," I said.

"She has no idea," Susan said.

We were quiet for a moment listening to the soundless distance between us.

"I miss you," Susan said.

"I know," I said. "I don't like this either."

"How soon?" Susan said.

"I got a guy to talk with tomorrow. Then maybe I can come home."

"Good."

"Who's with you now?"

"Chollo and Vinnie are downstairs in the study. Hawk is in the living room with Pearl reading the *New York Times* from this morning."

"I wonder who's reading to whom," I said.

51.

F RED SCHULER WAS still in business. He had an office on
Ontario Street, near the Justice Center. He must have been
doing okay because it was a nice office, with a reception area, in
a good building . . . with a secretary.

"Have a seat, brother," Schuler said.

He was tallish and lean with white hair and bright blue eyes.

"You had a job tailing someone named Bradley Turner," I said.
"In 1994. His wife apparently thought he was cheating on her."

"I tail a lot of husbands, for a lot of wives," he said. "And
that was a while ago. What's this about?"

"Murder case in Boston. I think this guy Turner killed a
couple of people. He was using the name Perry Alderson."

"How come you're involved?" he said.

"I was hired by one victim to check on the other."

Schuler nodded.

"And they both got killed?" he said.

I nodded.

"I feel like I shouldn't let clients get murdered without doing something about it," I said.

"You been a cop?" he said.

"Yeah," I said. "You?"

"Nope. I was an insurance investigator and sort of drifted into this. Mostly divorce work. Good money, a steady stream of clients. Not a lot of heavy lifting."

"Most adulterers aren't too hard to catch," I said.

"You got that right," Schuler said.

"How about Turner?" I said. "You remember him?"

"Not off the top of my head," Schuler said.

"You have files?" I said.

He grinned at me.

"Files and someone who knows how to use them," he said.

He went to the door and stuck his head into the reception area.

"Honey," he said. "You want to see what you can find in the files on a Bradley Turner, around 1994?"

He came back and sat down at his desk.

"Wow," I said. "This is like a private eye movie. A nice office, a secretary you call honey?"

"That's her name," Schuler said. "Honey Schuler."

"Relative?"

"Wife."

"Ah," I said. "She on salary?"

Schuler grinned again.

"No," he said. "I am."

Honey came in with a file folder and put it on Schuler's desk. She was attractive, stylish and silver-haired, with an ornate wedding ring. She smiled at me and went out.

"Married long?" I said.

"Forty-two years," Schuler said.

"And you like it."

"Being married?" Schuler said. "To her? Best thing ever happened to me."

He picked up the file folder and looked through it. I waited.

"Yeah," he said, "I remember this guy."

He took a photograph of Perry Alderson out of the folder and held it up. I nodded.

"That's him," I said. "How long were you on him?"

"About a month, I think." Schuler shook his head. "In my line of work you see some cockhounds, but this guy. Whoa! Different woman every day, sometimes more than one. Made me tired just watching him."

"Got pictures?"

"I don't know that it's good for business if I just empty out the whole bag for you."

"I know," I said. "What we say here stays here."

"Like Las Vegas," Schuler said.

"Sort of."

"No insult, but how do I know I can trust you?" Schuler said.

"You don't, but the other alternative is I make one phone call and the FBI will descend upon you like the wolf upon the fold."

"What's their interest?" Schuler said.

"One of the vics was an agent," I said.

Schuler was silent for a moment.

"And they don't know about me?" he said.

"Not yet," I said.

He smiled and took a smaller brown envelope from the folder and handed it to me.

"I've decided to trust you," he said.

"Oh good," I said, and began to look at the photographs.

It was Alderson all right, and a number of women, several of whom I'd interviewed, including Claire Goldin. Checking into hotels. Coming out of motels. Holding hands. Dining together.

"It's all coming back to me," Schuler said. "One of the babes made me. Brother was a cop. Cincinnati, maybe. Or Toledo, I don't remember which. He called me up and ragged on me. Wanted to know why I was following his sister. He made reference to coming to Cleveland and kicking my ass."

"And?"

"And nothing. I explained what I was doing. Promised not to include his sister."

"But you kept her photo?" I said.

He smiled.

"So maybe I'm not entirely trustworthy," he said.

"How did the case end?" I said.

"Right after that. Routine. I reported to Mrs. Turner. She paid me. Never saw either of them again."

"You didn't have to testify?"

"Nope. I called her once to follow up on that. Phone was no longer in service."

"You have her address?"

"The original one. I assume she moved."

"I'll take that," I said. "And her first name."

"Anne Marie," he said.

He wrote on a piece of paper and handed it to me.

"And the FBI?" he said.

"Mum's the word," I said.

52.

THE ADDRESS WAS in Laurel Heights, about eight miles out from downtown. It was a big Tudor revival house with a broad lawn, and a two-car garage, and a couple of big trees out front.

"My name is Spenser," I said to the woman who opened the door. "I'm looking for Anne Marie Turner."

I gave her my card. She looked at it, looked at me, and didn't invite me in.

"They haven't lived here for years," she said.

She was a big-boned blond woman who looked as if she might have grown up on a dairy farm.

"How long?" I said.

"Oh, God, when did we buy this house," she said. "Ten years. Eleven this summer."

"You bought it from the Turners?" I said.

"Yes," she said.

Then she smiled.

"Actually," she said, "not exactly. We bought it from the bank."

"The bank foreclosed?" I said.

"I guess. I don't know the details. My husband does most of the money stuff."

A cluster of small brown birds landed suddenly on the big lawn and began pecking about in the winter grass. I wondered what they found in there. Grass seed? Insects? Were they actually eating? Or just going through the motions? And did it matter. Maybe in the big scheme, but not in the small one I represented.

"Do you know why the bank foreclosed?" I said.

"Nonpayment, I assume," she said. "Phil told me we got a good deal."

"Phil is your husband?"

"Yes. Phil Karras. I'm Flora."

"Do you know where Anne Marie went?" I said. "Or her husband?"

"No," Flora said. "No idea."

"And the bank?" I said. "Do you remember the bank you bought from?"

"Sure."

She shifted a little. She was tiring of me. Hard to imagine. Maybe she was becoming aroused by my masculine profile and my Boston accent. Probably invite me in for coffee in a minute. That would be the giveaway.

"What bank?" I said.

"Workingman's Trust of Ohio," she said. "Right here in town."

I nodded.

"Is there anyone special you do business with there?"

"No. That's Phil's department."

I nodded. The birds herky-jerked around the yard pecking at whatever they were pecking. Of course, if she did invite me in for coffee, it would not be fair to accept. I was considering marriage. I waited. Now would be about the right time to propose the coffee, and prove it was desire, not boredom, that caused her to seem restless.

"Is there anything else?" she said.

Iron self-control.

"Is there anything else you can remember about the Turners?"

She shook her head.

"Not a thing," she said. "I never even met them."

"Thanks for your time," I said.

She smiled and closed the door and I walked down past the preoccupied birds to my car.

Hooray for Phil and Flora.

53.

THE SENIOR VICE PRESIDENT and chief lending offi-
cer for Workingman's Trust was a man named Norbert
Coombs, who looked like he'd been recruited from a bank com-
mercial. He was tall with thinning gray hair. His suit was a
dark pinstripe. His shirt was a blue Oxford. His tie was a small
blue bow tie with polka dots. His black shoes had wingtips. He
wore half-glasses, which he peered over with his head tilted as
he talked with me and looked at his computer screen.

"The Turners' last mortgage payment to us was on August
twenty-sixth, 1994," he said.

"And you foreclosed when?"

"March 1995," he said.

"You sent them dunning notices?"

"Every month," he said, "and according to the notations here, we called them, first monthly, then weekly."

He read off his screen some more.

"My predecessor went up to the home with the branch manager to speak to them personally. There was no one there and no sign that anyone lived there at all. The lawn wasn't mowed, mail had accumulated in the mailbox and on the front steps."

"Call the cops?" I said.

"Apparently," Coombs said, "they did. The Laurel Heights police reported the house was empty. That there was food, badly spoiled by then, in the refrigerator. Unwashed dishes in the sink. The phone had been shut off, but power and heat remained on. They cannot be denied a homeowner during winter months so that at least the pipes don't freeze."

"How much was the mortgage?" I said.

"A hundred and fifty thousand," he said.

"What was the house worth?"

"Maybe two hundred and fifty thousand."

"So they walked away from a hundred thousand," I said.

"Minus a broker's commission and a few fees."

"When you foreclosed on the house," I said, "what did you do with the contents?"

"It is bank policy to hold the contents in storage for a year, and then dispose of it."

"Sell it to a jobber?"

"Normally, or in some cases donate to charity, or"—he smiled and shrugged—"in some cases simply discard it."

"So the contents of the house from Turner's time are gone," I said.

"Yes, long ago."

"Do you keep an inventory?" I said.

"Normally we keep one for seven years before we purge it from the system."

"And are you faithful in your purging?"

He smiled.

"Probably not," he said. "It's not something I supervise closely."

"Could you see if you've still got an inventory?"

"Yes, excuse me for a moment."

He went out of his office, leaving the door open, and walked through the railed-off desk area, and talked to a skinny gray-haired woman at a desk near the railing. My guess was that status ran downhill as it got closer to the railing, and Skinny Gray Head was about as far down as you could get and be inside the railing. She diddled with her computer for a moment while Coombs watched over her shoulder and, after a time reached across the desk and took a printout from her printer and patted her thin shoulder and walked back up the status ladder to his office.

"Fortunately for your needs, Mr. Spenser," he said, "we have been neglectful in our purging."

He handed me a printout. I glanced at it and folded it in thirds and put it in my inside pocket.

"They have any savings, checking accounts here?"

Coombs consulted his computer.

"Yes. An interest-bearing checking account and a money market account."

"Do you have transaction records on those?"

More consultation.

"Both were emptied and have remained inactive."

"When were they emptied?"

"September seventeenth, 1994," he said. "Both. Same day."

"Can you tell who did the cleanout?"

"In a moment," he said.

He tapped some keys and waited.

"Both by check for ten dollars short of the balance," he said, and tapped again.

"So they wouldn't overdraw and call attention," I said.

"I presume so," Coombs said.

Tap, tap.

"We photograph the checks," he said.

Tap, tap.

"Both checks are signed Bradley Turner," he said.

I nodded.

"And you've heard from neither of them since?" I said.

"Not a word."

"Did he take the proceeds of his two accounts in cash?"

"Yes."

"How much?"

"Seventy-seven hundred from his money market account. Eight thousand and fifty dollars from checking."

"Would you just hand him the cash at the counter."

Coombs smiled.

"No, we're not that big a bank. I'm sure he gave us a couple days' notice."

"You didn't work here then?"

"No," he said. "I was living in Omaha at the time."

I stood and shook hands and slipped into my topcoat. Outside would be cold. Coombs's office had a fireplace. With a wood fire burning.

That's status.

54.

'M NOT AT all sure what Perry Alderson is up to," Susan told me on the phone.

"He's still coming."

"He's coming and he's talking," she said. "He's asked me to dinner once, and I made it clear that socializing would not be possible. But still he comes for his appointments."

"He's been very successful with women," I said. "He probably thinks, with you, it's only a matter of time."

"Probably," Susan said. "But there's more than that. He likes talking to me. He likes being with me."

"Me too."

"He may even like it that there is no romantic agenda available," Susan said. "A chance to relax."

"And a chance to talk about himself," I said.

"Yes."

"His goal is still to use you."

"I am well protected," she said.

"I know," I said.

"I feel like Hawk and I have become a couple," she said. "He sleeps in the spare bedroom. We have breakfast together in the morning. If you turn me down, I may marry him."

"If he'll have you," I said.

"There's that," she said.

It was dark out, and when I looked out the window all I could see was my own reflection. I didn't look old, exactly, maybe a little weathered, sort of. Like a guy who'd seen too many bodies. Heard too many lies. Fired too many shots. Swapped too many punches.

"He talk about stuff that would interest me?" I said.

"He talks mostly about his father," Susan said.

"What's he say?"

She was silent for a time. I could almost hear her sorting through what she thought she had a right to tell me.

"He has admitted that he sometimes uses his father's exploits in the counterculture, as if they were his. He says it increases his credibility and allows him to pursue his father's goals more fully."

"Credibility with whom?" I said.

"He brags that he is partnered with an international revolutionary enterprise."

"His language?" I said.

"Yes," Susan said. "An international revolutionary enterprise."

"He say how they are partnered?"

"He implied that they finance his part of the revolutionary enterprise," Susan said.

"Last Hope?"

"Yes."

"What do they get back?" I said.

"He says they like the prestige of associating with him, and implied that he was also a source of intelligence for them."

"As in spying?" I said.

"That was my understanding."

"Do you know the name of the people who help finance him?"

"No."

"Why would he tell you all this," I said. "This is very close to a confession."

"He cannot keep himself from bragging," Susan said. "From trying to impress me."

"And since you have a client-therapist relationship," I said, "your testimony would probably not be admissible, if it ever got to court."

"Probably not," Susan said. "And, if you are correct about him, he may think I'll not be available to testify against him."

"Does he ever wonder why I let him slide? Why I just don't blow the whistle on him and turn the tapes over to Epstein?"

"I don't know," Susan said. "I could speculate that he still assumes your goal is blackmail, and that if you turn over the tapes, you'll lose all the money you are trying to extort."

"That would be my surmise, as well," I said.

"Surmise," Susan said. "Do you speak more elegantly to me than to others?"

"Yes," I said. "Except sometimes."

"When you speak very inelegantly to me."

"Yes."

"At those times," Susan said, "I am a bit inelegant, myself."

"I'll say."

"I wish it were one of those times," she said.

"Yes," I said.

"Will you come home soon?"

"I got some cops to talk with tomorrow, and then, unless they open something up for me, I'll come home."

"Yay!" Susan said.

"You think he's telling you the truth about his father?" I said.

"He seems to be speaking of an actual person," Susan said.

"Feds looked pretty hard back along the counterculture path," I said. "You'd think if they came across a guy named Alderson they'd record it. Even if it wasn't Perry."

"His father's name was Brad," Susan said. "Bradley Alderson."

I was quiet for a moment.

"What?" Susan said.

"Before he changed it," I said, "Perry's name was Bradley Turner."

We were both quiet. I imagined the silence hovering above the small dark towns of Ohio and Pennsylvania, New York and Massachusetts.

"Which means what?" Susan said finally.

"Damn," I said. "I was hoping you'd know."

55.

THE LAUREL HEIGHTS police station was across the town square from an upscale shopping mall. It was like it was a detached part of the mall, with the kind of pseudo small-town America décor that you find in theme parks. I parked in a visitor's slot out front and went inside.

The cop on the front desk directed me to the detective squad room on the second floor. I sat down in a straight chair beside the desk of a detective named Coley Zackis.

"Name's Spenser," I said. "I called you yesterday."

We shook hands.

"After you called," Zackis said, "I got out the Turners' file."

He patted a thin manila folder on his desk.

"Not much," he said.

"You want to show it to me," I said, "or you want to tell me."

"You been a cop?" Zackis said.

"I have."

"Then you know what a file looks like," he said. "Be easier if I tell you."

"Illegibility is one of the first things you learn on the job," I said.

Zackis grinned. He was a heavy guy with a noticeable belly and thick hands.

"And you got to spill coffee on them," he said.

"What's in this one?" I said.

"Hardly enough to spill coffee on," Zackis said. "Turners stopped paying the mortgage. Eventually the bank sent somebody over there. Place looked deserted, so they called us. Patrol guys went up and took a look. Mail was piled up, grass wasn't cut, unopened newspapers all over the front walk. Phone was disconnected. They went in. No sign of life or anything else. It was like one day they just up and left."

"Bank inventories the stuff they left behind," I said. "I went over it last night. It looks like they didn't take much. No car."

"Couple of our detectives went up and looked around."

"You one of them?"

Zackis nodded.

"Yep," he said. "Just made detective at the time. We found nothing. There were still suitcases in a closet. His and hers. Makeup in the master bath. Couple purses hanging on a knob in the front hall closet. No way to know how many suitcases they had, how many purses. Makeup looked like it was used, but . . . you married?"

"Sort of," I said.

"How do you be sort of?"

"Takes practice," I said.

"Well," he said, "you probably know that your sort-of wife has more makeup than anyone would believe and that when she packs to go away she takes it all, but when you look at her bathroom, or wherever, there's, like, still a ton of makeup."

"I know that," I said.

"And you know she got a half-dozen purses."

"I do," I said.

"So we got no way to know what there was to start," Zackis said. "Did they take suitcases? Did she take a purse? Did she pack makeup?"

"Beds made?" I said.

Zackis glanced at the report for a moment.

"Nope," he said. "King-sized bed in the master bedroom was not made."

"People usually make the bed before they take a trip."

"So they don't have to find it unmade when they come back."

"Or have someone else find it so," I said.

"Like wearing clean underwear," Zackis said. "In case you're in an accident."

"Like that," I said.

"For most people the house is their biggest investment," Zackis said. "They don't just walk away and leave it."

"They left about a hundred grand on the table," I said. Zackis shook his head.

"It smells bad, doesn't it," he said.

"It does," I said.

"No signs of foul play," Zackis said. "No blood, nothing broken, no sign of forced entry. No hint of a weapon. Neighbors saw nothing."

"You put out a Missing Person?"

"Yep. Nothing. Not a peep," Zackis said.

"Neighbors shed any light?"

"Nope, pleasant couple," Zackis said. "She was a little older than he was. Both of them were friendly enough. Didn't bother nobody."

"How about the car?" I said.

"Missing," Zackis said. "Turned up a few months later in a parking lot at a mall in Toledo."

We were quiet for a time. At the next desk another detective, with his feet up, was cleaning his nails with a pocketknife.

"This ain't Cleveland, you know? Or Chicago. This is a little-city police department. Most of the time we get it done, but we don't have a ton of resources. Anne Marie Turner has a sister in Lexington, Kentucky. I actually went over there and talked with her."

He shook his head.

"Nothing," he said.

"Mail?" I said.

"Nothing," he said. "Bills, flyers, bank statements, no personal letters to either one of them."

"Credit card statements?"

"Usual, nothing caught your eye and after . . ." He looked at the file. "August twenty-sixth, no activity at all. He cleaned out both their bank accounts on September seventeenth."

"I know," I said.

"We haven't cleared the case," Zackis said. "But we haven't closed it either. Every once in a while, when it's a slow day, one of us revisits it, and comes up as empty as the rest of us."

I nodded.

"Ever hear of a guy named Perry Alderson?" I said.

"Perry Alderson," Zackis said. "I've heard that name somewhere. Perry Alderson."

He rubbed the back of his neck thoughtfully for a moment. Then he stood up.

"Lemme check something," he said.

Zackis went out of the squad room. The dick that was cleaning his fingernails looked at me.

"You private?" he said.

"Yep."

"How's that pay?"

"Not so good in this life," I said. "But in Paradise you get all the virgins you want."

He looked at me for a moment and then said, "I guess maybe I'll stay here, wait out my pension."

Zackis came back into the squad room with a piece of paper.

"I knew I'd seen the name," Zackis said.

He handed it to me. It was a Missing Persons circular on Perry Alderson with a picture, probably from a driver's license. I'd never seen him before.

"Erie police put it out," Zackis said. "Missing Person on a guy named Perry Alderson. Same year that the Turners went south."

"In Erie?" I said.

"Yeah."

"Nice memory," I said.

Zackis grinned.

"Made me think of Perry Mason," Zackis said. "I know a guy up there, want me to call him?"

"More than you know," I said.

56.

THE COP IN ERIE was named Tommy Remick.

"Alderson had a charter boat," he told me after Zackis handed me the phone. "Fishing. Sightseeing. That kind of thing. One morning it shows up empty, half aground near the marina where he kept it. No sign of him or anyone else. No evidence of foul play."

"When was this?"

"September thirteenth, 1994," Remick said.

"Alderson got any next of kin?"

"Ex-wife. Remarried. Lives in Stockton, California. Moved there around 1990 after she left Alderson. She hasn't seen him since."

"Nobody else?" I said.

"Nope. No kids. Parents dead. No siblings we can find."

"How old would he be?" I said.

"Born January 1957."

"So," I said. "He'd be forty-eight now."

"You say so," Remick answered. "I don't do math."

"If he's alive," I said.

"He isn't," Remick said. "Officially. It's been ten years."

"Twelve," I said.

"I told you about my math," Remick said.

"How big a boat?" I said.

"Another thing I don't know nothing about," Remick said. "Alderson lived on it. Was all he had. I think it slept four."

"So it was pretty big."

"You're thinking it might have been too big for whoever ditched it on the shore?" Remick said.

"Something like that," I said.

"If anyone ditched it," Remick said. "Boat could have just been abandoned and drifted in there."

"Prevailing currents?"

"Wouldn't prevent it from drifting in there."

"When's the last time anyone saw Alderson?"

"On the tenth," Remick said. "He was mopping the deck on his boat. Told the marina manager he had a charter that afternoon."

"Anyone see the charterees?" I said.

"The people who hired him? No. Nobody saw him leave," Remick said. "When the boat showed up empty we did a big search-and-rescue thing. Boats. Planes. Coast guard went all over the lake. We never found anything."

"How far from shore was it aground?" I said.

"Not far. Maybe twenty feet," Remick said. "Anyone wanted to ditch it would have had no problem swimming to shore."

"Motor off?"

"Yep," Remick said. "Plenty of fuel left. Only thing odd was, there was no anchor."

"Did he normally carry one?"

"They all do," Remick said. "He was a charter guy. People would sometimes want to anchor and fish, or picnic, or look at sunsets. He should have had an anchor."

"Any theories on that?" I said.

"If it'll hold a boat," Remick said, "it'll hold a body."

"Maybe two," I said.

57.

THE TRIP HOME from Cleveland on Route 90 took me north along the lake, through Euclid and Ashtabula, Ohio, and right past Erie, Pennsylvania. I thought about stopping in and looking at the lake where, I suspected, Bradley Turner had undergone a lake change and become Perry Alderson. But I missed Susan too much. And Pearl. I was beginning to miss Hawk. And I needed to get home before I started to miss Vinnie.

Cleveland to Buffalo was about three hours. Buffalo to Boston was longer than a trip to the moon on gossamer wings. It gave me plenty of time to catch up on my coffee, and think. The coffee was easier.

NOW *and* THEN

Certainly Alderson had once been Bradley Turner. Married to Anne Marie. Living in Laurel Heights. Taking some classes at Coyle State. Fooling around with a lot of the coeds, which was probably why he took the classes. No one had found any sign of paid employment, so he probably depended on his wife's money, which seemed substantial: nice house, nice suburb. For whatever reason, maybe because she caught him fooling around, one day he had taken the missus on a cruise out of Erie and while out there had killed the wife and the boat guy, and, maybe, tied the bodies to the anchor and dumped them in the middle of the lake. It was a big lake. Then he had taken the boat back to shore and, either to avoid observation or because he didn't know how to dock it, he had run it aground, swum to shore, gone back to his car, and driven off into the sunrise. Probably with Perry Alderson's ID in his pocket.

I stopped at a travel plaza near Batavia. Got gas, used the restroom, bought coffee and a nourishing cinnamon bun in the crowded food court, and went back to the thruway. The leisurely days when Howard Johnson's was your host of the highways were but a quaint memory.

So he gets back in his car, in his wet clothes, and drives on back home, like nothing happened. He takes all the money out of the bank. He's smart. He doesn't get greedy, try to sell the house, or the car. He drives the car up to Toledo, parks it in a mall, takes the bus back to Cleveland. He takes nothing from the house that might connect him to Bradley Turner. Then as Perry Alderson he goes to Cleveland, probably, gets a place to live, and starts creating a new persona for himself. By 1996 he's counseling people in shelters, and ten years later he's a professor at Concord College, and a lecturer on matters of individual freedom. Is it a great country or what? That's why he lied about his age, I thought. It wasn't just vanity. Alderson was younger. Maybe he'd actually done, as Turner, the things he claimed to have done as Alderson. Or maybe his father had done them. Or maybe he'd made them up. Maybe he'd made the father up. He had, after all, made himself up.

I stopped near Syracuse for more gas and coffee. The travel plaza was packed. It was a Thursday in early December. Where the hell was everyone going? More existentially, where the hell was I going. I took my coffee to the car and continued east.

I was going home.

58.

T HE HOMECOMING FESTIVITIES were intense and extended, and Pearl was visibly annoyed at being shut out of
Susan's bedroom for so long. It was three o'clock in the morning when she was able to join us. Susan had a bottle of Laurent-
Perrier pink champagne, and we drank some of it, sitting up in
bed, with Pearl sprawled between us.

"Whew!" Susan said.

"Whaddya think?" I said. "Love or lust."

"For us," Susan said, "it's a meaningless distinction."

"For everybody?"

"If they're lucky," Susan said.

"Like us."

"And they work at it," Susan said.

"Like us," I said.

"Sometimes it's been hard work," she said.

"And sometimes no work at all," I said.

She nodded and sipped her champagne and looked at me over the rim of the glass. To be looked at by Susan, naked, with those eyes, over a glass of pink champagne, was all I knew on earth, and all I had to know.

"What are you thinking?" she said.

"Keats," I said.

She smiled.

"Truth is beauty, beauty truth. . . ?" she said.

"Something like that."

She kept smiling.

"Only you," she said. "After hours of carnal excess with the girl of your dreams . . . thinking about Keats."

"I'll bet other people think of Keats," I said.

"Oh, I'm sure, probably right in this neighborhood . . ."

"If carnal excess occurs in Cambridge," I said.

She ignored me.

"But none of those thinking of Keats look like you," she said.

"Their loss," I said.

"And their companions'," Susan said.

Pearl rolled onto her side and stretched out full length, which took up a considerable amount of bed space. Probably revenge.

"Do you know what you're going to do about Perry Alderson and all of that?" Susan said.

"I'm thinking about it."

"Are you going to tell Epstein what you've learned?"

"I'm thinking about it."

"Why wouldn't you tell Epstein?" Susan said.

"I'm thinking about it," I said.

"And you do not plan to discuss it with me tonight."

"Exactly," I said.

I filled my champagne glass and reached across Pearl to pour for Susan. She drank some. I drank some. We looked at each other. Pearl's breathing was the only sound. Susan reached across the dog and traced one of the scars on my chest. There were several.

"It's just a scar," she said. "Just a kind of physical memory."

"Yes."

"It doesn't hurt," she said.

"No."

"It did," she said.

"True."

"But now it doesn't."

"Are we getting metaphorical?" I said.

She smiled again and nodded.

"Yes," she said.

"This, what we have," I said, "is an earned relationship. Of course there would be scars."

"And the time when we were separated? When I was with somebody else?"

"That's a big scar," I said. "But it's also when we both did the most to earn what we've got."

"You truly know that?" she said.

"I do. I've never liked it much, but I know what we got from it."

She continued to trace the scar on my chest. Then she looked at me again. Her eyes were luminous.

"No pain, no gain," she said.

59.

Y OU GOT ENOUGH," Hawk said. "You give what you got
to Epstein and he can run Bradley Turner down. They
good at big searches."

"I know," I said.

Susan was working. We were in the spare room. Chollo was
asleep on the couch. Vinnie was listening to his iPod and doing
something with the trigger sear of a Rugar brush gun. Hawk
and I were sipping coffee and watching Susan's door.

"Hell, with what you got, and they work with the Cleveland
cops, sooner or later, they gonna find something," Hawk said.

"Erie too," I said.

"Uh-huh."

"Makes sense," I said.

"And then we can stop hanging round here, watching Vinnie clean the weapons," Hawk said.

"I know it," I said.

"So," Hawk said. "You going to see Epstein today?"

"Not today," I said.

"When?" Hawk said.

"I'm thinking about it," I said.

Hawk nodded. Today's snack special was raspberry turnovers in a cardboard box. Hawk stood and walked over to the table and selected a turnover from the box. He looked at me. I nodded. He selected another one and came back and handed it to me, and sat down with his. In silence we ate our turnovers and drank our coffee and looked at Susan's door. Vinnie got the sear and trigger reassembled and flexed the trigger gently and nodded to himself and continued with the reassembly.

"Russell Costigan," Hawk said.

"Russell Costigan," I said.

"Guy Susan ran off with back then."

"I know who he is," I said.

"We both know this about him."

I shrugged.

"We both know you couldn't kill him like you wanted," Hawk said.

"Wouldn't have taken me where I wanted to go," I said.

"So you sat on it," Hawk said. "But it didn't go away; and now here's Doherty. Wife runs off with someone turns out to be a bad man, and this time it gets him, and her, killed."

I didn't say anything.

"Maybe I'm just looking for justice," I said.

"Maybe you looking for revenge," Hawk said.

"Maybe they're the same thing."

"Now you thinking like me," Hawk said.

"Uh-oh."

"So we both know Alderson did them, or had them done. Whyn't you just shoot him and get it done?"

"Because I'm not like you," I said.

"Tha's right," Hawk said.

I looked at him. He smiled.

"I need to get him the right way," I said.

"Tha's right," Hawk said.

"Lemme think about it," I said.

60.

STAYED WITH the rest of the posse in a state of high readiness while Susan had her fifty-minute hour with Alderson or Turner or whoever he really was. When they were through and he had uneventfully gone, she came into the spare room. She was in her understated, for Susan, shrink garb. Today it was a dark blue velvet blazer over designer jeans.

"Anything?" I said.

"Interesting," she said. "Nothing that can't wait. I have my next client in a minute."

"Can you give me a one-sentence slug line, on 'interesting'?"

"I think there's some kind of masturbatory mental sex going on," she said.

Vinnie turned his head to look at her. Chollo smiled. Hawk showed nothing. Which was what Hawk always showed.

"In whose mind," I said.

Susan grinned at me.

"I have a Harvard Ph.D.," she said.

"So, only in his mind," I said.

"Exactly," Susan said.

"You think he's still trying to seduce you?" I said.

"I think he thinks he has."

"Which is why he keeps coming?" I said.

"He has not forgotten that he wants to use me against you."

"But the tail has begun to wag the dog?"

"Maybe," she said.

"And the fact that he has to walk past us when he arrives?" I said.

"Half the fun," Chollo said.

We all looked at him.

"You are his enemy," Chollo said. "If he can walk past you on his way to having mind sex with the *señorita* . . ."

"*Ay, caramba,*" I said.

Chollo smiled.

"*Sí,*" he said.

All of us stared at Chollo. Except Vinnie, who might have been sleeping, or might have been listening to his iPod, or both.

"How you know that?" Hawk said.

"It is a trick we hot-blooded Latins often play in my village," Chollo said.

"There's probably a lot of that going on where you live," I said.

"*Mucho,*" Chollo said.

"And part of my charm, for him," Susan said, "is that he gets to strut past you and have his imaginary way with me, and strut back out, under, so to speak, my protection . . ."

She looked at her watch.

"You have other charms," I said as she started across the hall.

She turned and her smile gleamed with possibility.

"And don't you forget it," she said.

61.

BEHIND CAPTAIN QUIRK'S desk in the kind of new offices of the Homicide Unit was a picture of a very young Ted Williams, in a Minneapolis Millers uniform. He was beautiful. Nineteen years old then, and it was all ahead of him.

"I need a safe house for Susan," I said.

"And you think I'm a general contractor?" Quirk said.

"Three, four days," I said, "keep her safe. At least four guys."

"You and Hawk aren't enough?"

"And Vinnie," I said. "And a guy from LA named Chollo."

"The four of you?" Quirk said. "Not enough?"

"We have something we have to do," I said.

"Legal?"

"No."

"So you want me to aid and abet you," Quirk said, "in an illegal action, by protecting your girlfriend at taxpayers' expense while you're doing it."

"Yeah."

Quirk sat quietly for a moment. His thick hands rested motionless on his desk. His nails were manicured. His shirt was very white and very starched. He had on a dark blue tie with maroon stripes. A brown/black corduroy jacket hung neatly on a hanger on the coatrack in the corner.

"You get a Tommy point for balls," Quirk said finally.

I nodded. We sat.

"Susan know about this yet?" he said.

"No."

"Because if you can't get her covered you can't do what you want to do," Quirk said.

"That's right."

"So first you gotta find out if I'll buy in," Quirk said.

"Yes."

"Got to do with the deal you're working on with Epstein?"

"Yes."

"So?"

"Don't trust them," I said.

"He's pretty good," Quirk said. "Don't let the appearance fool you."

"I know. It's not him I don't trust. I don't know what his troops are like."

Quirk nodded.

"Susan's in real danger," Quirk said. "You wouldn't ask me if she weren't."

I nodded. Again we were quiet.

"I can't assign people," Quirk said.

I waited.

"But I can probably get a couple volunteers. Frank Belson will do it. Lee Farrell."

"Need at least four," I said.

Quirk shook his head.

"Settle for three," he said.

"The third being. . . ?"

"Me," Quirk said. "After office hours."

I nodded.

"Two guys, and you, make four anyway," I said.

"'Specially if the other two are Belson and Farrell," Quirk said.

"I owe you," I said.

"You do, but I probably owe you, too," Quirk said. "And I remember what you did for Frank when his wife was missing. You got a plan?"

"As a matter of fact, I do."

62.

A T 10:48 on Monday morning a guy in a green Toyota dropped off a woman in front of Susan's home. The woman wore a red snap-brim hat and sunglasses and a long black coat. She came up the front steps and into the front hall. Susan came to the office door to greet her.

"I'm Susan Silverman," she said.

I came out of the spare room.

"Detective Moira Mahoney," she said.

We shook hands and went into Susan's office. As always when Susan had a patient, the louvered blinds were half closed on both sets of windows so that no one could see in. Moira put her purse down, took off the hat and the long coat and the shades, and laid them on Susan's couch. She didn't really look like Susan. Few people do. But she was the same size and shape and general coloration.

"You know the plan," I said.

"Quirk laid it out quite carefully," she said.

"Who drove you over?" I said.

"Lee Farrell," Moira said. "He's going to wait outside."

"Alone?" I said.

"Frank Belson is up the street in another car," Moira said.

"Good."

"Thanks for doing this, Detective," Susan said.

"Pleasure," Moira said. "Got some coffee?"

"Sit down," I said. "I'll get you some."

I got coffee from the spare room. When I came back, Moira was in the client chair and Susan was behind the desk.

"You'll need to stay here until eleven," Susan said.

"Sure," Moira said.

"Want a free shrink?" Susan said.

Moira smiled.

"Can I get a rain check for my husband?" she said.

Susan laughed.

"And how will you get home?" she said.

"Somebody can drop me in Central Square," Moira said. "I'm parked in the Cambridge Police lot."

"Will I see you later?" Susan said.

"Nope. I'm just here for the head fake," Moira said. "Then back to normal duty. I don't even know where you're going."

"Too bad," Susan said. "A woman would be nice."

"You got Lee," Moira said.

"He's been with me before," Susan said. "I don't find him womanly."

Moira smiled.

"It's Lee's joke," she said. "On the ride over here he said that's why he always gets this duty."

"Lee's pretty good at being gay," I said.

"The best," Moira said.

I stood at the front window looking out between the slanted louvers. After a time, Hawk came into the room. Moira looked at him like an aardvark at a termite mound.

"You're Hawk," she said, "aren't you."

"Yes, I am," Hawk said.

"I've heard about you."

"All true," Hawk said.

"If we finally bust you," Moira said, "I hope I'm in on the collar."

"If you not," Hawk said, "I have you paged."

Moira smiled.

"Please," she said.

Hawk looked at me.

"Car here," Hawk said.

"Farrell driving?"

"Yeah."

"Any sign of Belson?"

"Nope."

"There wouldn't be," I said. "He'll be there. Vinnie and Chollo where they're supposed to be."

"Yeah."

"Okay," I said. "Time for you to go out on the front porch and lounge on the railing and catch some air. When the woman comes out you pay her no attention."

"You already tole me that," Hawk said.

"Oh good," I said. "You remembered."

Hawk went. I looked at my watch. Twelve minutes past eleven o'clock.

"Okay, toots," I said to Susan. "Get into your disguise."

She smiled and nodded and put on the long coat and the wraparound shades.

Susan paused and looked around her office for a moment.

"It won't be long," I said.

She nodded.

"Be very, very careful," she said.

"Yes," I said.

She put her arms around me and kissed me. I put the red hat on her head and tilted it over her face the way Moira had worn it coming in.

"My hair," Susan said.

"You can fix it when you get there," I said.

"Yes," she said. "I can."

We looked at each other for a moment, then she turned and went out the door past Hawk, who ignored her, down the steps, and got into the passenger side of the green Toyota beside Farrell. They drove away. Hawk remained where he was taking the air happily. Not a care in the world. Seeing everything that moved on Linnaean Street.

63.

AFTER A PROPER interval I drove Moira Mahoney up to Central Square and went on into Boston, parked on a hydrant on Beacon Street, and walked down across the Common to Locke-Ober's on Winter Place.

Epstein was at the bar in the foyer when I got there. He had a Gibson in front of him.

"Nice to see you again," he said.

"Always seems too long," I said. "Doesn't it?"

"Yeah. What have you got?"

"You're ahead of me," I said. "Lemme get a drink."

He nodded. I ordered. The bartender brought it. It was a quiet afternoon at Locke's bar. Later, people would come in and have a cocktail while waiting to be seated, but at 5:10 in the afternoon there was only one guy, reading the *Wall Street Journal* and nursing a Gibson.

"You got anything?" I said.

"We've gotten a look at Alderson's finances," Epstein said. "He's got about a hundred and forty thousand in a money market. No checking account. No savings."

"Better than I'm doing," I said.

"True," Epstein said.

He poked the pickled onion around in the bottom of his glass.

"Odd that there's no checking account," I said.

"True," Epstein said.

He got the onion just where he wanted it in his glass and sipped a little of the drink.

"The bothersome thing," he said, "is that the only activity in the account is at the end of each month, when his paycheck from Concord gets automatically deposited."

"How long?"

"Account was opened with a thousand dollars two years ago," Epstein said. "He has not withdrawn anything, which is why it's up to a hundred and forty thousand."

"So what's he live on?"

Epstein shook his head.

"Speaker's fees?" I said.

"Most of those gigs are free," Epstein said. "Very few pay much."

"And he's got an expensive condo, and a nice car, and he employs a driver."

"So where's it come from?" Epstein said.

"Is that a rhetorical question?"

"Sadly, so far," Epstein said, "no."

"I have a theory," I said. "But first let me give you what I know."

"I like a case when people start saying *know* instead of *think*," Epstein said.

He gestured for another drink. The bartender brought it and looked at me. I shook my head. I didn't mind getting drunk with Susan, but I didn't want to show up that way. Epstein poured his still uneaten onion into the new drink and the bartender took away the empty glass.

"His name isn't, or wasn't, Perry Alderson," I said. "It was Bradley Turner."

"That his original name?" Epstein said.

"Don't know," I said. "Probably."

"*Probably* is better than *maybe*," Epstein said. "Where'd he get the name, obit notice?"

"Better than that," I said. "He killed the original Perry Alderson."

Epstein drank some of his Gibson.

"Just to steal the name?" he said.

"No, it was involved with killing his own wife, the late Anne Marie Turner."

"You prove any of this?" Epstein said.

"You will," I said. "I'll give you enough stuff to investigate. It'll be only a matter of time."

Epstein turned in his stool so that his back was against the bar. He held his Gibson in both hands in front of him.

"Go," he said.

I gave him everything I had, except the part about Alderson having mental sex with Susan. It took a while, and Epstein didn't interrupt me once. He sipped his drink carefully. Otherwise he just sat and listened and didn't move. As I talked, the bar began to fill. Men in suits, mostly. A lot of them pols down from the state house, just across the Common. When I finished, Epstein took a last drink from his Gibson, and held it in his mouth for a moment before swallowing. Then he tipped the glass up and his head back, and got the two onions, which he chewed and swallowed.

"So he's old enough in fact," Epstein said when the onions were gone, "to have been in all that counterculture boogaloo that he claims."

"Probably," I said.

"It's an area the bureau covered exhaustively," Epstein said.

"Because they were such a threat to national security," I said.

"You know it," Epstein said. "They were giving aid and comfort, for God's sake, to our enemies."

"Who were?"

Epstein grinned.

"I forget," he said.

"I think it was the commies," I said.

"Oh, yeah," Epstein said. "Them."

"Eternal vigilance," I said.

"Sure," Epstein said. "Anyway, if he ain't in our files, he didn't exist in the sixties. Can you write down names and places and dates?"

"Everybody but one," I said. "I implied to the PI that I wouldn't give him to you."

"Professional courtesy?" Epstein said.

"Actually I threatened him with you if he wouldn't talk to me."

Epstein nodded.

"Do I need him?" Epstein said.

"I don't think you will," I said. "He's solid enough. But if you do need him to make your case, I'll give him to you."

Epstein nodded.

"Your word's good," he said.

"Mostly," I said.

Epstein smiled slightly.

"I think you should put a tail on Alderson," I said. "Open or not, that's up to you. But this thing is going to blossom pretty soon, I think, and we wouldn't want Alderson to disappear again."

Epstein nodded.

"You got plans you're not sharing with me?" he said.

"I do," I said.

Epstein thought about that for a moment and then shrugged.

"So far so good," he said.

64.

ON TUESDAY MORNING at 9:50 Alderson came strolling into Susan's office and found me there, with my arms crossed, leaning my hips against the front of Susan's desk.

"What are you doing?" he said.

I didn't say anything.

"Where's Susan? Dr. Silverman."

I didn't answer.

"I have an appointment," he said.

I said nothing.

"All right. I don't know what game you are playing but I haven't the time nor the patience."

He started to turn.

"Wait a minute," I said and stood up.

He turned back toward me and I hit him with a left hook. It was the left hook I'd been working on with Hawk for years. The left hook that if I'd had it as a kid Joe Walcott would never have beaten me. The left hook I'd been saving for a special occasion. It was a lollapalooza. I felt all of me go into the hook. I felt it up my arm and into my chest and shoulder and back. I felt it in my soul. It was almost like ejaculation.

Alderson staggered back against the wall to the right of the door and sank to a sitting position. He wasn't out, but bells were ringing. His eyes were unfocused. He felt sort of feebly around on the floor as if he were trying to locate where he was. I went back to the desk and leaned my hips on it again and folded my arms, and waited. Slowly his eyes refocused. He stared at me. And in his stare I saw for the first time the furtive reptilian glitter of his soul.

"You used to be Bradley Turner," I said. "You killed your wife and a charter boat captain named Perry Alderson and stole his identity. You are employed by an outfit called FFL to acquire information."

The reptilian gaze didn't waver.

"So the price of silence has now gone up," I said.

He didn't say anything.

"I want one million dollars by tomorrow, in cash, or all of this goes to the FBI."

He kept looking at me as he slowly got his feet under him and slid upright against the wall.

"We had a standoff," I said. "What I had would cause suspicion but you could have survived it. Now you can't. If the Feds don't bust you first, the FFL will kill you to cover its tracks."

"Is Dr. Silverman aware of this?" he said.

"Tomorrow," I said.

"I'd like to know if she was merely a part of your plot against me," he said.

"I don't care what you'd like," I said. "You need to deliver the money by tomorrow. You want to set a time and place, I'll be here."

I thought for a moment that he might bite me. But he didn't. He gathered himself and straightened his shoulders and after a moment of venomous staring, he turned and left the office. In the hall, Hawk opened the door for him, and closed it after him. I walked to the spare room and watched as Alderson walked up Linnaean Street toward Garden.

"You want it all, don't you?" Hawk said.

"All," I said. "Alderson, FFL, anybody who surfaces along the way."

"You think he'll come up with the million?"

"No."

"You think he going to make a date to deliver," Hawk said, "and show up with some shooters?"

"I do."

"And we gonna be ready for them?"

"We are," I said.

Hawk grinned.

"And maybe we be lucky," Hawk said. "And Alderson show up with the shooters and you got to kill him?"

"I'm going to roll this up," I said. "I have to kill him, I will."

"You already ratted him out to Epstein," Hawk said.

"Double coverage," I said. "I don't want to wait for them. Until it's done Susan can't live her life."

"You, me, Vinnie, and Chollo," Hawk said. "You need anybody else? Maybe Tony give us some people."

"We'll be enough," I said.

"Hell, you and me enough, babe," Hawk said. "Everybody else just lighten the load."

"There's a lot on the line here," I said. "I think I'll stick with the old favorites."

65.

I N THE EVENT that Alderson and company didn't bother to
make an appointment, I went to sleep on top of Susan's bed
with all my clothes on. At 2:12 Hawk came in and woke me.

"They here," he said.

I rolled out of bed. Put the Browning on my hip, stuffed two
extra magazines into my pocket, and followed Hawk downstairs.

We went into the spare room. There were no lights on.
Chollo stood at one side of the front window looking out
through the open louvered shutters. In Susan's office, at that
front window, I could see Vinnie dimly in the ambient light
from the street. Vinnie had an assault rifle.

"Chollo taking a little tour," Hawk said. "Spotted them."

"They make you?" I said.

"I am more stealthy than the Mexican jaguar," Chollo said. He continued to look out the window as he spoke.

"So they didn't make you?"

"Of course not."

"Tell me about it," I said.

"They arrived in a van," Chollo said. "No markings. I count six. They have all been seeing many movies, I think. Black clothes, faces blackened."

"I like the look," Hawk said.

"Guns?" I said.

"Handguns, of course," Chollo said. "I spotted at least one automatic weapon. An Uzi, I believe."

"Where are they now?" I said.

"Around the house," Chollo said.

"They don't know that Susan's not here," I said. "And they need to get us both."

"Doors are locked," Hawk said.

"But not impenetrable," I said.

"How nice," Hawk said.

"Two ways for them to go," I said. "Back stairs up to the porch off Susan's kitchen, or through the front hall here and up the front stairs."

"I'd do both," Hawk said.

"Yes," I said. "Me too. Chollo, you and Vinnie take upstairs. Off the kitchen. Hawk and I will lie in the weeds down here."

Vinnie had already started up the stairs.

"I want one of them alive," I said.

Chollo smiled.

"Play it safe," Chollo said. "You get one alive. We get one alive. You don't need two, I'll shoot one."

"Fine," I said. "You see any sign of Alderson?"

"Sadly no," Chollo said, and followed Vinnie up the stairs.

"They have jaguars in Mexico?" Hawk said.

"I don't know," I said. "Why don't you take Susan's office? They come through here, we'll catch them between us."

"Okay," Hawk said. "But shoot careful. I don't want you to shoot me."

"You shoot," I said. "I'm going to grab one."

66.

IN SUSAN'S SPARE ROOM, where I stood, with the louvers closed, the silence merged with the darkness, so that each seemed more intense than it otherwise would have. The dim nocturnal glow of streetlamps, moon, and stars drifted in through the glass panels in the front door, and made things faintly visible in the hallway. But Hawk, ten feet away from me in Susan's office, was perfectly invisible.

The darkness was thick and close.

I was holding a sawed-off baseball bat. A Manny Ramirez model. I kept my 9mm Browning on my hip, with a full magazine and a round in the chamber. No sound came from upstairs where Chollo waited with Vinnie. No sound came from Susan's office where Hawk waited with his big .44 Mag in a shoulder holster, holding a sawed-off, twelve-gauge double-barreled shotgun.

I went to the front window and looked out through the shutter. Nothing moved on the street. No traffic. No cars with the headlights on and the heater going while the driver listened to late-night radio in the warm car. No couples coming home from a late party, holding hands, looking forward to intimacy.

The quiet was stifling.

From the back of the house came the faint sound of glass breaking. It wasn't much. They'd probably taped it first. Then more silence. Then maybe the hint of a latch being turned, a door being opened. Then silence again. Then, suddenly, a dim movement in the front hall. One man, carrying a handgun, dressed in black, his face blackened. He went to the front door and unlatched the safety bar and opened the door. Two more men came in. One had an Uzi. They too were all in black. The two men started silently up the front stairs. The first man, the man who had let them in, checked to see that the door was unlocked and then closed it and turned and started to follow the other two past me where I stood in the spare room.

I stepped out behind him as he passed and brought the sawed-off baseball bat down on his gun hand. He yelped softly and the gun clattered on the front hall floor. The noise was shockingly loud. The men on the stairs turned. I grabbed my guy by the hair and yanked him into the spare room. The man with the Uzi sprayed the hallway with bullets. As soon as he stopped shooting, Hawk stepped out of Susan's office and killed both men with the shotgun.

In the office I had my man on the floor with my knee on his chest and the muzzle of the Browning pressed hard against the bridge of his nose. Hawk dropped the shotgun, took out his handgun, and went up the front stairs past the two dead men without making a sound.

On the floor in the spare room, my guy was perfectly still, disoriented, probably, from the suddenness of his situation. For several moments there was no sound. Then there was a rattle of gunfire from upstairs. Then there was nothing. Then there was the sound of footsteps on the front stairs, and Hawk's voice.

"We got one too," Hawk said.

67.

WE FOUND THE van keys on one of the dead men. Vinnie pulled the van up beside Susan's house and we put the dead men in it, being careful about fingerprints. With Hawk behind him, Vinnie drove the van up to Porter Square and left it in the parking lot at the shopping center. Then he came back with Hawk.

It was approaching four in the morning. The lights were on in the house. The brightness seemed almost overpowering in contrast to the stark blackness before. My captive sat on the couch in the spare room. I sat in front of him with my handgun resting on my right thigh. Chollo was with the other captive in Susan's office.

Both the captives were younger than I had expected. Mine was barely more than a kid. Maybe twenty-two. He had a slim, athletic build, like he might be a good tennis player. His dark hair was shoulder length and his big dark eyes were terrified. It had probably been a great adventure for him. And now it wasn't.

Hawk and Vinnie came back from Porter Square. Hawk came into the spare room with me. Vinnie went to prowl the house, in case there was another attack. Which there wasn't. Hawk sat down off to the side and looked at the kid with interest. I put my gun away. Neither of us spoke. The kid tried for the calm fatalism of a true terrorist. But he didn't have it. He stared back at us for a while.

Then he said, "What are you going to do?"

Neither Hawk nor I spoke. Even in motionless repose, there was something electric about Hawk, a sense of barely contained kinesis. The kid's attempt at stoicism kept breaking down into uneasy glances at him. The silence extended.

"I am a prisoner of war," the kid said.

Hawk and I did not respond. The silence became increasingly palpable. The pressure became more dense. The kid's face was very pale. He seemed to have some trouble swallowing.

"If you do not kill me," he said, "I can tell you things."

"Do," I said.

"Excuse me, sir?"

His voice was thin and shaky. It sounded as if his mouth was very dry.

"Do tell us things," I said.

"I . . . I will tell you whatever you wish," he said.

"Who sent you here?" I said.

"Perry."

"Perry who?" I said.

"I don't know his last name, sir. We only use first names. He is a brother in arms. He is the leader of Last Hope."

"You?" I said.

"I am Darren," he said. "I am a member of Freedom's Front Line."

"Why did Perry send you?"

"We were to kill you and the woman," he said.

"Why?"

"You were a threat to the movement."

Darren's voice was stronger, as if talking about something gave him a sense of involvement in his fate.

"What movement?" I said.

"The people's war on despotism."

"Who else is in it?"

"I will tell you who I know, sir, but I don't know many, just the people in my cell."

"And Perry," I said.

"Yes, sir. Perry found me in a wallow of depravity, sir. He helped me see the truth about American life. He saved me from addiction and dependence. He helped me find purpose."

"He find you in a shelter?" I said.

"Yes, sir."

"That his job?" I said. "Recruiting for the movement?"

"No, sir. That's just how he is. He tries to save people."

I nodded.

"So what does he do for the movement?"

"He's an intelligence source, sir. He's very adroit at getting valuable information."

"From women," I said.

"That is often the case, sir."

"Did you help kill Dennis Doherty?" I said.

The kid's head sank forward some.

"Yes, sir," he said.

"At Perry's request?"

"Yes, sir. I am a good soldier, sir."

"You're a jackass," I said and stood up.

The kid flinched at the movement, and glanced at Hawk. I went out of the room and across the hall. Chollo was sitting behind Susan's desk, with his feet up, and his gun on the desktop beside him. Our second captive sat stiffly in the chair that Susan's patients normally used. He didn't move when I came in.

"Geoffrey," Chollo said. "Says he's a soldier in the war against despotism."

The second captive was no older than mine. He was shorter, and a bit pudgier. He sat rigidly, as if movement would hurt.

"Who sent you?" I said.

Geoffrey looked at Chollo. Chollo smiled at him and nodded encouragingly.

"Perry," Geoffrey answered.

"Tell me about him," I said.

Again he looked at Chollo.

"Tell him, Geoffrey," Chollo said.

Geoffrey nodded stiffly and told me the same story Darren had told.

"And I'll bet you met him at a shelter," I said.

"Yes."

I nodded.

"Okay," I said to Chollo. "Bring him across the hall. I'm going to call Epstein."

68.

B Y THE TIME Epstein arrived with his hordes, it was just me and the freedom fighters, Hawk and company having silently departed. By the time the hordes finished up and went away with the two prisoners, it was quarter to seven in the morning and the sky was growing light. Epstein and I were having coffee at the counter in Susan's kitchen.

"Susan's okay," Epstein said.

"She wasn't here."

"Happy coincidence," Epstein said.

I nodded.

"The two zombos tell me that there were other men here," Epstein said. "And that four of their zombo companions were killed."

"Really?" I said.

Epstein nodded.

"Good coffee," he said.

"Better than Shauna's," I said.

"Hard to be worse," he said.

I went to the refrigerator and opened the door and looked in. It was very clean.

"You want a bagel?" I said. "Susan doesn't have too much else."

"Too early," Epstein said. "I eat this early I feel lousy all day."

I closed the refrigerator door. Epstein sipped some coffee.

"Here's what I think," Epstein said. "I don't say I'm going to try to prove it. I'm just sharing my thoughts."

I nodded, and sat at the counter.

"I think you set this up. You got Susan to spend the night somewhere safe, and then I think you did something to force Perry Alderson's hand, and he responded and you were waiting for him. Hawk was probably here, and Vinnie Morris, and I don't know who else."

I nodded.

"In a while," Epstein went on, "four bodies will turn up somewhere with nothing to tie them to you but the word of two whack job terrorists, who will probably find it in their best interests not to talk about it anyway."

I nodded. Epstein poured himself some more coffee and added some milk and a lot of sugar.

"In doing so," Epstein said, "you have behaved like a reckless vigilante."

I nodded.

"Which has resulted in a great saving in time and effort on behalf of the bureau, and may have been of service to your country."

"Gee," I said.

"So I think I will just say *fuck it* on the question of who else was here and who was killed, and concentrate on arresting and prosecuting Alderson, and the FFL."

"Seems a sound decision," I said.

Epstein nodded.

"I'm going to go arrest Alderson," he said. "You want to come along?"

"Nope," I said. "I've had my moment with him."

Epstein nodded.

"Good," he said.

69.

GALVIN CONTRACTING SERVICES had come in and re-placed the broken glass in Susan's back door, and patched the bullet damage, and would be back tomorrow to paint. It was early afternoon, and Susan and I were drinking pink champagne in her office. She was at her desk, I sat on the couch.

"Doctor," I said, "my problem is that I'm in love with a shrink."

"That's my problem, too," she said.

"That you're in love with a shrink?"

She smiled.

"No," she said, "that I'm the shrink."

"I'm rarely in here," I said.

"I know."

"Why are we in here now?" I said.

"Some impulse toward reestablishment, I guess."

I nodded.

"Romance is difference," I said.

"Excuse me?"

"John Updike said that, or something like it, in a short story. We're drinking pink champagne in your office in the middle of the afternoon. It's different."

"Yes," she said. "I see that."

"Have you ever made love on this couch?" I said.

"Not yet," she said.

We sipped our champagne.

"He sat here and flirted with me," Susan said, "and talked about his father."

I nodded.

"And of course it almost certainly wasn't his father. It was himself when he was Bradley Turner."

"What Epstein's found out so far," I said, "would suggest that. Bradley Turner was active in the antiwar counterculture."

"The child is father of the man," Susan said.

"Or something," I said.

"He was so filled with ego and need and self-regard that he had to talk about himself even at the risk of exposure."

"So he pretended the self was someone else," I said.

"Someone he admired," Susan said.

"And the flirtation?" I said.

"He had been so successful," Susan said, "with so many women, for so long. I think he couldn't believe it would fail. Even when it was quite clear that I was not succumbing."

"That's why he kept coming?" I said.

"He kept coming, in part, I think, because he so enjoyed talking about himself."

"To you," I said.

"Yes."

"You're a splendid person to talk with," I said.

She smiled.

"It is my profession," she said.

"It is also your nature," I said.

She inclined her head to thank me, without committing to whether I was right or not.

"And as noted," Susan said, "in his relationship with me, he had the illusion that it put him one up on you."

"So that his seduction was, in a sense, successful from his perspective."

"Mind fucking," Susan said.

"You Harvard grads," I said.

She smiled.

"He must have been horrified to find you here when he came for his session."

"Yes."

"And you hit him," Susan said.

"Really, really hard," I said.

She emptied her glass. I poured more for each of us.

"Has Hawk shared his theory with you?" she said.

"About my identification with Doherty and how Alderson fills in for Russell Costigan?"

"Yes."

"He has," I said.

"What do you think?" she said.

"That was then," I said. "This is now."

"So he's wrong?"

"I don't know that he's wrong," I said.

"And how do you feel now that you've avenged Doherty's murder, and destroyed Alderson?"

"Pretty good," I said.

We each sipped our champagne. The pinkness didn't have much to do with flavor, but it certainly was pretty. And different.

"Is it a good time to talk about marriage?" Susan said.

"The medieval courtly love tradition holds that love is impossible in marriage because it is coerced," I said.

"And what do you think of the courtly love tradition?" Susan said.

"I think it's bullshit," I said.

"Me too," Susan said.

"So maybe we should recline here together on the couch and consider alternative theories," I said.

"What a very good idea," Susan said.